The Girl in the Tower

To my parents, who taught me to read, and who supported my addiction to literature.

CONTENTS

ACKNOWLEDGMENTS

I want to throw out my thanks to all those amazing people who read the original manuscript again and again (and again). A few people specifically: Munger, for supporting my anxiety-induced habits (and being the other half of my schizophrenic self); Mr. Cox, for fixing my computer and saving countless words; Mr. Sorensen, for inspiring me to write, and teaching me how; Rachel and Jen, for being my biggest supports, demanding each page as it was finished; my family, who understood why I was always lost in my writing. Also, a big round of applause and a basket of cookies to the lovely Kylee Ann, who drew the cover, and Allison, who's always been honest about whether or not I suck.

The Girl in the Tower

Emily Elizabeth Nelson

PROLOGUE

Rampion was not a common plant, but it tasted quite good, so it probably wasn't surprising to my father when my mother developed a hunger for the leaves. Denying a woman with child any food was dangerous, so the measures he went to were understandable. And really, what was the risk? The witch had such a large garden, how could she notice one small plant missing?

Perhaps she wouldn't have noticed if it had been a one-time thing, if my mother had recognized the danger and quieted her pleas for the stolen produce. But every time my mother ate a piece of the rampion, her hunger grew, like a giant beast waiting to tear my family apart.

She was seven months along with me the night my father got caught.

I can picture the scene: the witch, Jacqueline, standing above my father in rage as he trembled in absolute terror beneath. He undoubtedly thought that he was going to die. As he begged for his life, Jacqueline would have interrupted him to strike a deal: his life and the rampion for his unborn child. What went through his head at the moment can only be guessed at.

I don't blame him for his decision, but perhaps he blamed himself. What he felt when Jacqueline took me away and my mother dropped dead of grief could only have been despair. He was left with no family and he had no friends, isolated from the most of the town by a river that flowed through the dark forest, twisting wildly. There was no one to comfort him as he mourned.

I was not to learn any of this for a long time. Not even after I went to live in the tower did Jacqueline tell me even the tiniest bit of information. I didn't know it then, but it would take a series of life-changing events before I would learn my story.

Now, looking back on everything, I still find myself a tad confused. Over time, details have been blurred, left out. As the story passed by word of mouth, it soon became nothing more than a mere fairytale.

CHAPTER ONE

Deep down, I had always known that Jacqueline wasn't my real mother. She treated me like her daughter–her precious Rapunzel–and I loved her like I would have loved my mother, but I knew that I was adopted. I was a foundling, like in my books. It wasn't really a bad thing to me, but I was constantly reminded that I was different when I looked at Jacqueline.

She had long, straight red hair, the trademark of a witch, with pale clear skin. I had once tried dyeing my hair red with raspberries when I was eight years old. Little did I know that the fruit wouldn't turn my hair a color anywhere near the hue I so desired. All that I had gained from that was a week of stained hands and bright pink locks.

Jacqueline was also quite short. I never knew how tall she was, but I was five foot seven inches by the time I stopped growing, and she was several inches shorter than I. Somehow, she always managed to tower over me.

Still, I loved her as my mother, for she was all I had. She had the warmest hugs and the brightest smiles. She always made me feel like the most important person in the world. Of course, our world was very small.

For the first many years of my life, we lived in a little cottage in the woods. It only had a few rooms, one of which was our shared bedroom. I didn't mind. Sometimes I wished that my bed was a bit bigger, or the straw inside it a bit less pokey, but I was happy. Our life was simple, but that was the way I liked it, and Jacqueline made sure that we always had the basic necessities.

We had a small garden where we grew corn and carrots, potatoes and lettuce, but we still had to go to the village occasionally. Jacqueline let me tag along when she went. I loved those rare trips; they were some of the few changes in my otherwise constant life.

One year, in the midst of winter, we were snowed in. We couldn't get to the village for supplies and our food was running out. The situation frightened me. I was on my bed, playing absentmindedly with my doll, trying not to think about the rumbling in my stomach when Jacqueline came in, holding a rock about the size of her fist. She asked me what I wanted most of all to eat. I shrugged and when she kept pressing me, I answered that I would like an orange, my favorite food. She rubbed the rock in her fingers and even as I watched, it became the fruit I desired. Until the snow melted, Jacqueline used spare odds and ends to keep us fed.

People came to visit often, more likely than not coming to ask for the cure of one ailment or another. Most of the time, I preferred to sit in the garden and weave rampion flowers into my hair. I liked the light purple petals; they were different from the other flowers. They were special, like me.

Sometimes I did stay inside to watch the guests. Secretly, all I wanted was to see Jacqueline work magic. Then, late at night, I would sit up in my room, trying to recreate the same effect. Once I had seen her turn a toad back into a man. I had really wanted to learn that one. I thought that maybe if I could turn the toads in the forest into children, there would be someone who would not exclude me from their games. The village children avoided me, but I wanted so desperately to play with them. It never occurred to me that perhaps the reason I wasn't welcomed into their groups was not solely because of me, but because of my guardian who held so much power.

I never could figure out how to make a friend from a toad, so I had to content myself by watching the guests. A few incidents stuck in my head.

One man came in with a sack of beans that he claimed were magic. He held the bag up to my face, whispering of giants and beanstalks. The talk had excited me, but Jacqueline didn't like what he was saying. She threw him out so fast one might have thought he had grown wings. "Nonsense," she muttered to herself as she slammed the door.

Another time, a man came, dragging a boy about eight, my own age. The man let the boy go and explained about a horrible curse on his head. He spoke in a loud voice, his words flying out of his mouth like arrows. The village wanted him gone. Him or the curse, one had to go.

As the man talked to Jacqueline, the boy wandered over to me. I was sitting at the kitchen table, fidgeting with my hair. It was past time for lunch, and I had still not eaten. I stared at him, unwilling to speak first.

"My name's Sven," he offered, meeting my eyes defiantly.

"Rapunzel." I was more intent on getting food than meeting this dark haired, light-eyed boy. There was something about him that I disliked, but I couldn't quite decipher what I was feeling.

"That's an odd name."

"No, it's not!" I countered, all thoughts of food banished. I jumped off my bench and glared at him. No one could withstand my glares.

Except this boy. Sven wrinkled his nose at me. "You have funny eyes too."

My light green eyes were a source of vanity for me. They were the same color as the leaves of my namesake, a color that no one else had.

With a "humph," I turned my back to him. For a moment neither of us spoke, and then I felt a tug on my hair.

"Ouch!" I spun around, angry. "Why'd you do that, you dummy?" I shouted.

Sven shrank back. "I just wanted to touch it," he mumbled.

He wasn't the only one. My hair reached my waist and was a source of wonder for many people in the village. Most grown women's hair didn't even reach their shoulders. Many asked in awe if they could touch it.

"Boys are so dumb," I pronounced, folding my arms angrily. My scalp stung.

Sven's face went red, and he tugged my hair again, harder this time.

I struck out at him, my arms waving in the clumsy anger of a child. One fist hit him on the nose, sending him sprawling.

Jacqueline took away my dessert for a month, but I decided it was worth it.

It was barely one year later that an even stranger event occurred.

I was lying in the garden, picking lazily at the turnips. Their fluffy leaves were fun to play with. Jacqueline had gone to the village. It was one of the few times that she hadn't taken me. She was meeting with the man in charge of the boy, Sven, to try and see if she could lift his curse.

A sudden shadow fell over me. I tried looking up, but I was on my stomach and had to roll over before I could see.

A man with a wild mop of blonde hair stood quietly, his hands grasping a cap in front of him. He had a prickly face, as if he hadn't shaved in a while. A brown knapsack rested on his back; it showed the same amount of wear as his rumpled clothing. His hair struck me as the most peculiar. It was just like mine. I could never get it to behave. It stubbornly resisted taming of any kind.

The man didn't speak. Instead, he just looked at me like he would never look away. Uncomfortable, I squinted up at the sun. I had forgotten that it hurt my eyes to do so.

After another minute, the man broke the silence. "Hello there, little one. What are you called?"

"Rapunzel," I said shyly. I glanced around briefly, though not quite sure what I was looking for.

"Rapunzel," the man repeated. "Rapunzel." He seemed to taste the name, as if deciding whether or not he liked it. I hoped he would. For no reason at all, I longed for his approval. "What a beautiful name."

"Thank you, sir." The words that tumbled out of my mouth surprised me. I usually had a hard time being polite.

The man smiled. He had a warm smile. It made me want to smile too. "Who do you live with here?" he asked, sitting cross-legged beside me.

"Jacqueline," I said simply.

"Is she your mother?" He bit his lower lip, seeming to regret asking as soon as he did.

"No, but she's nice to me and I love her."

He looked relieved at my answer. "You are happy, then? You like living with Jacqueline; she is kind to you?"

"Yes," I said. His questions were plentiful and odd, but the man seemed nice.

"Why don't you take a walk with me? Where is Jacqueline?" He stood slowly.

"She's at the market in the village." I stood too, dusting dirt off my dress. "She's buying pumpkins and she promised me that we would make a pie later." The thought came to me that maybe the man could join us. I didn't think to ask his name. It didn't really seem important.

We started to walk around the edge of the garden. It was not large and would probably only take five minutes to walk, a little longer than that, perhaps. The man walked slowly. He seemed to be in no hurry. As we walked, my hand found his. It was large, easily enveloping my small fingers, and was covered in calluses—a reassuring hand.

"What do you like to do, Rapunzel?" he asked softly.

"Play with the flowers. They make good crowns. They make me feel like a princess. I like to climb trees and listen to the birds. They sing pretty songs. Sometimes I sing with them." I said this all in a rush.

"Would you sing a song for me?" the man asked.

"Yes," I said. Singing made me happy, and I wanted this man to be happy too. I sang one of my favorite songs.

"I saw a robin in the road
It sat quite still beside a toad.
The robin, with its feathers red,
Hopped upon the toad's green head
How silly did this seem to be?
Oh, what a sight for one to see."

The man laughed a loud booming laugh. "That was very good. What about other children? Don't you play with the children in the village?"

"No, they don't like me. They pull my hair. I play by myself and with a dog that comes to our house. I even have my very own doll," I said proudly.

The man seemed sad for a moment, but the sorrow passed. "A doll? Well, that's very good. What does she look like? Does she have hair like yours?"

We continued on to the house, the man asking questions about me. I hoped that the man would stay for a while. Sometimes people did that; we had a spare room in the cottage.

"Will you be my friend?" I asked.

"Why yes, Rapunzel. I'd like that," he said.

"Oh good, I have two friends now: you and Jacqueline," I said happily.

A tear ran down the man's face, but before I could ask what was wrong, a voice came from across the garden.

"Rapunzel!" It was Jacqueline. She ran towards us, jumping over cabbages and carrots. She reached us quickly, slowing to a stop in front of the man. She looked at him in surprise.

"Emmanuel." She blinked, and then her look hardened. I shrank under the ferocity of it, though it wasn't directed at me. The man, Emmanuel, held her gaze.

"Madam Gothel," he said curtly. "You look well."

"Rapunzel, go back to the house," Jacqueline said quickly. "Now."

"But–" I started.

"Now!"

Startled, I let go of the man's hand and scurried away. I didn't go back to the house, however, heading instead for the garden wall and climbing it. I leaned my ear to the cold stone. Snatches of conversation drifted my way.

"I know, but I had to see her. I…" Emmanuel's voice got too faint to hear.

"You have no right!" Jacqueline's voice was loud, angry.

"I have every right. Do not presume to tell me what I can and cannot do." Emmanuel didn't raise his voice. He didn't need to. He seemed to make his point as effectively in a soft voice as he would've in a loud one.

They argued like this for a long time. I eventually went to the house. It had gotten dark and I was tired. Not too long after, Jacqueline stormed in.

"Rapunzel," she called. "Pack your things."

I came out of my room, confused. "Where are we going?"

"We have to leave. Quick, get your things together." She hurried about packing clothes, pots, and books into her bag.

"Why? I don't want to go."

"I'm sorry, but we have to."

"No." I stamped my foot. "I don't want to go."

"Rapunzel, you will pack your things right now, or you will spend the rest of your life grounded!" Jacqueline shrieked, eyes wild.

She never yelled at me, and suddenly I was scared. I started crying.

My tears caught Jacqueline's attention. The anger faded out of her eyes and she seemed to realize how greatly she had frightened me.

"Oh, Rapunzel, I'm sorry. I'm so sorry, don't cry dear." She sank to her knees beside me and stroked my face until I calmed down.

"Why are we going?" I whispered, hiccupping slightly.

"It's not safe for us here anymore. Come, my dear." She gathered me in her arms and waved her hand. All my things were suddenly packed in a traveling bag. "Come, let us find a new home, won't that be exciting?"

I nodded slowly, not quite sure.

It was exciting. At least it was for the first three times we changed houses. We didn't stay in any one place for long. Sometimes I thought I'd caught sight of Emmanuel, but I couldn't be positive. My usually impeccable memory failed me when it came to Emmanuel. I remembered him, but I somehow couldn't think of his face or what he had said to me.

Jacqueline grew more and more panicked. Every time we moved locations, she got another gray hair, another wrinkle. She didn't stay very still anymore; she twitched a lot. It worried me. Sometimes I would go and sit with her to make her feel better.

When I was twelve, we found the tower. It was in the middle of the woods and the room in it was about sixty feet up. A large window faced east with smaller windows on the other three sides. What it was originally intended for, I couldn't even fathom.

With her magic, Jacqueline furnished the largest room with kitchen supplies, a fireplace, food, a bed, and above all else, books–hundreds of books on every subject.

When the time came for me to go up, Jacqueline squeezed my hand. "I need you to be strong, Rapunzel. This is the only way to keep you safe from the evil ways of the world," she said.

Tears in my eyes, I nodded and took her hand as she led me up the winding stairs. Once I was up, Jacqueline used magic to close the stairs. They disappeared. I had no way to leave the tower.

Three rooms: one main room, a closet, and a room for bathing and using the toilet. That's what my world had shrunk to. Nothing else mattered.

"I am living in a small house not far away. I will come and visit you often. I'll even bring more food with me," Jacqueline promised, cradling my face in her hands.

I didn't respond, and with a sigh, she crossed to the window. Pain danced across her face. As the years had gone by, it had become harder for her to perform magic. She gasped as she lifted off the floor and gently floated to the ground.

I fell onto my bed. My world had become a prison. I tried to make the best of it. How different was it from before, really? I had never had friends in the village. This couldn't be that big of a change, could it?

I soon found out that the tower wasn't at all like my old life.

CHAPTER TWO

The sun pulled at my eyes, inviting me to wake up. A bird perched itself nearby and began to sing its little heart out.

"No," I half-groaned, half-mumbled. "Go away, it's too early." I pulled a pillow over my ears and eyes. If I couldn't see the sun, then it hadn't risen yet.

The bird sang louder. With my eyes covered, I thought it might be a mockingbird. I peeked out from underneath my pillow to check. Sure enough, a small, black and white mockingbird rested contentedly at my window, singing as if to wake all of the woods.

By now I was too awake to go back to sleep. I slowly sat up and looked around. Everything was the same as it had been when I had gone to bed, which was disappointing. I had always slightly hoped that the furniture would move around as it seemed to in so many of the different books I had read.

If it was secretly moving around, it always managed to settle back into its normal positioning.

I had spent six years in the tower with no one but Jacqueline for company. It wasn't an awful life, just a very lonely one.

Standing slowly, I wandered to the mirror on the other end of the room. Shiny green eyes and a tangled mess of blonde hair reflected back.

My hair had grown longer than I had ever thought possible. With her magical powers fading, Jacqueline had come up with a new way for her to visit me. Every night I drank a potion to make my hair grow. By now, it had to be at least seventy feet long. It dragged behind me everywhere I went. The potion made the hair long, thick and even stopped it from getting dirty, but I still couldn't manage to control it enough to wrangle it into a proper braid.

The wavy golden strands hung free until they reached my elbows; there they were hastily stuffed into a braid. It had taken two days for me to painstakingly knot it all. My hair simply didn't want to stay still. It was worth it though. At least it wasn't constantly catching on to every little thing anymore.

For all it was a hassle, however, I still loved it. When the sunlight hit it just so, I felt more than beautiful: I was stunning. Today, as I looked in the mirror, I wasn't too dissatisfied.

I slowly changed out of my nightgown into a dress. Normally I would have worn slacks, but today was my eighteenth birthday, a special occasion on which Jacqueline insisted I wear a dress.

I crossed to the window and looked out. I couldn't see Jacqueline, but I didn't worry. She was always a little later than she planned.

As I looked back at the mockingbird, it sang out a simple melody. Using the same notes, I quickly composed a short ditty.

What happened to the little bird?
It sings so loud by all it's heard.
Once there came a cat along
It followed slyly the sweet bird's song,
The bird still sang, for it knew not,
That by the cat, it would be caught.
Alas, the cat thought he would win,
For the bird had not seen him,
When, to the cat's surprise,

The birdie leaped into the skies.

I laughed at myself. It was a silly song, but I couldn't come up with anything that wasn't funny, or even anything that made sense for that matter. All my songs were just made up of rhyming lines. Nothing came close to the lyrical proclamations of the songs in my books. I'd have to work on that, maybe in some of my spare time. It wasn't as if I was lacking time to myself.

A voice called out from below. "Rapunzel, Rapunzel, let down your hair!"

I looked down and there stood Jacqueline, carrying a bag on her back.

Grinning, I quickly wrapped the beginning of my braid around a hook by the window, carefully leaving enough slack to avoid my hair being pulled from my scalp. Then I draped the long braid out the window. It tumbled to the ground. Jacqueline grabbed the makeshift rope and climbed up with the agility of someone much younger.

"Rapunzel, happy birthday." She embraced me. Her presence made me warm on the inside.

"Oh, thank you. It doesn't feel very special. I'm just the same as I was yesterday." I hauled my hair back up, unhooked it and followed Jacqueline to the kitchen table.

"Rapunzel, that's a sad thing to say on your birthday. Why don't you cheer up? Look, I bought you a present." She set her bag down and pulled out a wrapped gift. She handed it to me carefully, as if it might break.

Just as carefully, I removed the paper. Underneath laid a box, not very deep or wide, but long.

"A box. Just what I've always wanted," I said as I picked it up and examined it. It was white wood, unpainted and unadorned.

Jacqueline just chuckled and shook her head. She was used to my antics.

I lifted the lid off the box slowly and gasped. It was a necklace, a beautiful creation. It was made of green and purple glass beads that ran up the sides. In the middle was a larger glass pendant, yellow in color, with white stripes reaching out in a sunburst pattern. It sparkled even without much light. I couldn't tear my eyes off of it.

"It belonged to my great-grandmother. It's got its own magic," Jacqueline said.

I looked up at her. She knew how much I loved and longed for magic. When I was younger I had held fast to the hope that I was a witch. I knew that my blonde hair meant I couldn't be–witches always had red hair–but I was constantly asking Jacqueline if I had become magical yet.

"It's wonderful; it's perfect," I said breathlessly. "What kind of magic?" I picked it up gently.

"As long as you have it, you will always be able to find the one you love." Jacqueline took it from my hands, and clasped it around my neck.

Immediately, I felt a warm glow from where Jacqueline was standing. I closed my eyes and spun around. The warm feeling stayed with Jacqueline. "It works," I said in awe. "I'll wear it all the time."

"And you are so beautiful wearing it." Jacqueline reached into her bag once again.

But for whom? I thought. *Who was there to look beautiful for except Jacqueline?* The thoughts made me sad, for the answer was nobody. There was nobody to see me but Jacqueline.

"Rapunzel, darling, I have to go now. I'm preparing to leave on a brief journey, and I won't be back for a week. You'll be fine without me, now won't you?" She looked genuinely worried for me. She always was.

I laid my hand on top of hers to reassure her. "Of course, I'll be fine," I said. "And if something goes wrong, I can always call on a brave prince to save me," I added in an attempt to lighten the mood.

"You do not need a prince, you have me!" Jacqueline snapped.

I opened my mouth, but decided against what I had been about to say. I did not want to fight. "Yes, Jacqueline. As always, you are right." I went back to the window, wrapped my hair around the hook and let it down once more.

Jacqueline descended and faded into the forest. For the second time that day, I hauled my hair back up and let out a sigh of relief. Her visits had become more and more stressful. She was so resentful if I even hinted at being lonely. She couldn't understand why her company wasn't enough.

I had the whole day to myself now though, and first thing I did was trade my dress for a tunic and a pair of wrinkled slacks. I sighed, much more comfortable. I didn't understand why Jacqueline insisted that I wear gowns. I did not like them one bit.

I gathered together supplies and started to make a cake. That's what normal people did on their birthdays, or so my books told me. I mixed the ingredients together and stuck the result hastily in my stove. The fire made the room hot since it was a bright spring day, but that simply couldn't be helped. I opened up a few of my smaller windows. A light, teasing breeze blew through.

I grabbed a book off my shelf at random and sat down on my bed to read it. Quickly, I glanced down to see what I had grabbed.

It was the tragedy of two lovers who fell under the spell of an evil troll. Jealous of the feelings the two shared, for he knew that he could never love, the troll cursed them to never speak to each other again. They could no longer make a sound. As miserable as the couple was, the hardest to bear was the loss of their singing voices, for the two were the best singers in the land.

Sighing, I settled down and opened the cover. Like many of my books, this tale was beautifully illustrated. The first picture showed the two holding hands. They faced away from the viewer, so I couldn't see their faces.

"No happily ever after for you," I whispered.

It was true. In the end, both died without ever having spoken again.

At least they had each other. I skimmed through the book, stopping briefly every few pages. I knew the story well and all too soon, I reached the end. I closed the book with a snap, not sure if I wanted to feel melancholy at the tragic end of the characters, or to gag at the sappiness of the narrative.

I went with the second. Bearing my own isolation was easier if I rejected all alternatives. If I accepted my situation as the most fortunate, I found that I was much happier.

Taking a look around the room, another book caught my eye. It lay on the ground, alone and discarded.

The book was dark green with gold stitching. It was almost two inches thick, the parchment heavy and yellowing. It must belong to Jacqueline. A few years ago, she never would have slipped up like that. Now however, with her nerves so obviously frayed, she had become forgetful.

As I approached it, I glanced around furtively. I laughed after I did that. Who was there to see me? Gingerly, I picked the book up. Gold words sparkled across the cover:

Buchen von Zauber

I stared. I knew enough to know what it said. The Book of Magic. The book was written entirely in the old language, but I had studied it quite a bit and there was much that I could pick out. "Cloak of Invisibility… Levitation… Imperious Spell…" Words seemed to jump off the page as I flipped through.

Why would she be carrying this with her? I wasn't sure. Something caught my eye. One of the pages had a corner folded down. I turned there and stared at the words for a moment before I could decipher them. "A Boundary Spell," the glistening words said. I reviewed the instructions, trying to figure out some of the more obscure words.

It was a spell that would basically set up an invisible wall over any surface. The wall could be made impenetrable or you could make it so a person might enter via a magical object.

What would Jacqueline be doing with a spell like that? What possible use could it be to her?

I read through the spell again and found that a word had been scribbled carefully in between the lines. At first I thought that it was written in a completely foreign set of runes, but on second glance I realized something.

"Idiot," I said to myself. I simply turned the paper over. The word was just written on the other side. I stared at the word. "Hair." It didn't really make sense. What did she mean?

I looked at my hair.

"Wait," I breathed. Could my hair be magical in and of itself?

I shut the book carefully; I would investigate more later. A cloud of dust rose off of it. With only a slight hesitation, I opened the book back up and closed it quicker this time. A bigger dust cloud rose and settled slowly.

As I set the book down, I remembered the cake I had left. It had just finished and would start to burn soon. I took the pastry out of the oven and ate it slowly, relishing every bit. With the book of magic resting by my side and the cake in front of me, I sighed happily. Perhaps this week alone without Jacqueline wouldn't be so bad after all.

CHAPTER THREE

It was day two of Jacqueline being gone. I had never been left by myself for over three days. The prospect of another five days promised more excitement than anything in a long time.

Today it was raining as if it would never stop. I listened contentedly to the drip-drop of rain on the roof. I relaxed on my bed, hands clasped behind my head, eyes closed.

Drip drop.

Rain is falling.

A performance for the world.

Drip drop.

Thunder booming,

Great drum rolls in the sky.

Drip drop.

Lightning flashing,

Bolts of light are hurled.

Drip drop.

People watching,

Planting time is nigh.

It was an old song, traditionally sang in the village during the springtime, right before the crops were planted.

I pretended that I could see the village planting. It had been many years since I had been a part of it, but I could still envision what would be going on. The men would've gotten up early to plow, pushing and grunting, turning the ground over and over. Later, still before the sun rose, the women would come out with small pikes to make holes in the ground.

It was my job to put the seeds in the hole and pat the dirt back over it. I wandered out with all the other children to do so; we often raced each other to see who could go the fastest. It was the only time I was accepted by others my own age.

I think that the key difference was my hair. Most other days it was allowed to hang loose, but on planting day, it was pulled tightly back in a bun to keep it from dragging in the dirt. With my hair gathered up, I stood out less from the villagers with their cropped, chin-length locks.

The rain brought me back to the present. I opened one eye and glanced around. All my candles had blown out with the wind, and only two lanterns remained lit. Their sparse light flickered in the strong gusts of wind.

A lightning strike sent me jumping out of bed and the accompanying clap of thunder found me leaning out the window, ignoring the fact that I was getting soaked, and straining to see the next bolt.

When the sky lit up again, I saw something strange in the distance. A dark figure in a large cloak rode astride a big animal I couldn't quite identify. I thought for a moment. I did know what it was: a horse. There were pictures of those in my books. There had never been any of those in the village; they were far too poor for that.

The horse switched directions several times rapidly, as if the rider couldn't decide which way to go.

On the not-so-distant horizon, another bolt struck. Almost immediately afterward, thunder boomed. The tower shook, as did many of the taller trees. The horse reared up onto its hind legs, twisting madly. The figure flew off and the horse ran away.

By now it was once again too dark to pick anything out. I left the window, a disturbed feeling deep in the bottom of my stomach. What would happen to the figure on the horse? A better question came to my mind: Why did I care?

The thought made me sad. Was I really so mean-spirited? Perhaps I was. I had been living in a tower for six years with the company of only one other person. Considering the circumstances, I was probably lucky that I didn't laugh at the mysterious figure's predicament.

The tower shook a little, as if agreeing. *Yes,* it seemed to be saying. *You're heartless. You're horrible.* The flashes of lightning confirmed the truth of it.

"Oh shut up." I collapsed onto my bed and threw a pillow over my head. I fell asleep like that. When I woke, the rain had been joined by hail.

Thwack. Thwack. Thwack. No more soft droplets to sing to me, the small pellets bounced off the roof with force that far exceeded anything that would make sense considering their size.

I held my hand out the window to catch some of it.

Bad idea.

"Ouch!" I screamed, jerking my hand back in.

There was now a welt on the back of my hand about an inch in diameter. I shook it, as if that would help make the sting go away.

I had imagined that my week alone would be relaxing and enjoyable. Figures that it would be cold and I'd injure myself.

No, I thought, *injure wasn't the right word, it wasn't that bad. More like hurt.* I tried to stop thinking. I was getting far too insane talking to myself. *I wonder where Jacqueline is.*

The magic necklace invited me to find out. I clasped it around my neck, closed my eyes and waited. A strange feeling came over me. There was the same warm feeling as before, but this time I thought that I could almost see where Jacqueline was. Everything was fuzzy and after a moment, I lost the vision. Just the warm, tingly feeling was left.

"That was weird." I had read somewhere that talking to yourself was the first symptom of madness. "Great," I said to the wall. "Now I'm going mad."

Thunder clapped. Now it was just mocking me. I stuck my tongue out towards the window and laid myself down to go to sleep.

When I next awoke, it was day three of my complete and utter isolation and I had nothing to do.

I pursed my lips and grabbed the Book of Magic. This time, I noticed an author's name below the title: Ian M.

Wroon. I'd never heard of him, not that that was surprising or anything.

I flipped through, not interested enough to pay any attention. I ruffled the pages and let them fall where they wanted. The book opened to a page written not in the spidery black handwriting that covered everywhere else, but in thick red ink. It looked like blood.

POWER

A voice inside me screamed, *Stop. Close the book, set it down, and walk away. Something is not right! You do not want to know what this says.*

As always, I ignored the voice. Anyway, what harm could a grouping of words do?

"It's been a matter of some concern for many generations that a witch's power often declines over time," the book said.

That was Jacqueline's problem! I read on.

"It is widely believed by the most renowned of philosophers that there is no reverse to this. However, though my studies are often dismissed as trivial, I have indeed found a way to equate the diminishing of power."

What I read next worried and scared me. Wroon spoke of how to elevate one's power. It involved the deprecating of the most important part of a person: their soul.

It seemed like a horror novel. Multiple murders and giving up your soul were essential to completing the spell. I recoiled in revulsion and pushed the book away. It fell off my bed and closed. I was momentarily relieved. I didn't want to touch the book ever again.

I didn't move from bed the rest of the day. The unknown figure stuck to my mind. Questions buzzed around my head like bees. *Who was he? Why was he out in a storm? Where was he now?*

I blinked. Why did I automatically assume the rider was a man? It could have been a woman. No, I felt sure that the rider had been a man. Perhaps I just liked the idea of a man nearby. It seemed exciting and mysterious.

"Agh, Rapunzel! Stop it; you've got to get a hold of yourself!" I thumped my head against my pillow. Thump. Thump. Thump. It didn't really make me feel better.

Boom, thunder sounded, laughing heartily.

I looked out from underneath the pillow. The first thing I saw was the book. It was open to the page that said "Power" again. I had not opened it.

In a panic, not quite in my right mind, I leapt off my bed, grabbed the book, and with all the strength I could muster, I flung it out the window. It hit the muddy, wet earth with a slap.

"Oh no," I breathed. "That was bad. That was very bad." I bit my lip as my mind raced. I tried to will the book to magically fly back up. It sat stubbornly on the ground.

I had planned on letting Jacqueline find the book in the same spot she had left it. She would ask me if I had touched it, and I, using my superior acting skills that I had had all this time to polish would say, "Oh no, Jacqueline. I knew that it belonged to you, so I left it alone. That is what I was supposed to do, is it not?" I was excellent at feigning the sweet innocent little girl that Jacqueline still saw me as.

But now… now what was I supposed to do? The never-ending rain would destroy the book within a few days. I could imagine the pages stuck together with moisture, the glue dissolved, the binding falling apart.

Would Jacqueline be upset, or angry? I thought about the spell of power. The red ink would be oozing between the mud splattered pages like blood. With a shudder, I decided that she would be angry. She wanted her power back more than almost anything. I recalled one day a few years ago when Jacqueline had been fantasizing about being as powerful as she once had been.

"Madam Jacqueline Gothel. It would be spoken in every household. 'She is the very best. There is not a thing she cannot do!' They would flock from miles around just to see me," she said, her eyes closed, envisioning how it would be.

"Of course they would," I agreed, though not entirely convinced that this was a realistic dream.

"And you, my dear, they would come to see you. They would come to admire and envy your beauty." She opened her eyes and glanced out the window and around the tower. "Best of all, you could leave. Think of it. With my powers, I could protect you. We could go and live somewhere nice."

"Could we go back to the village?" I asked.

She never did answer me. She shut her eyes once more and seemed to drift off into a world of her own.

Now I had made up my mind. I started to search frantically around the tower. There had to be something to get the book back up here, something, somewhere.

Wait. My common sense suddenly kicked in. I did not want to get the book back; it was far beyond my repair skills. There was no way that I was going to get that book all the way up to the window without it falling apart. No, there had to be a different way to correct this mistake; there had to be an efficient way to erase this little mishap. My head drooped. That wasn't possible. I was going to be found out. All chances I had of ever leaving the tower were slowly disappearing.

Destroy it. The thought came to my mind unbidden and unwanted. *You could just destroy it. Pretend as if you had never ever seen it in your life. She won't blame you, how could she? How would she know that it had not fallen out of her bag earlier, or later? She would think that it was lost forever. She would never trace it back to you. Not you, her perfect little girl.*

I rushed to the window and shot my gaze downward. The rain was doing its job well, but not well enough. What I needed was for all the water to concentrate in one place.

That would be easy. I grabbed one of my large pots that I usually used to make stew. I went and set the pot under the mouth of the water pump.

This was one of the things that I couldn't live without. A pipe ran all the way down to a well in the ground. Jacqueline had explained how the pump worked, but I couldn't remember anymore. Not like I had ever understood.

I filled the pot up about halfway. There was no point in filling it completely. I wouldn't be able to carry it if it was filled up to the top. I had learned that lesson the hard way.

When I was satisfied, I lugged it over to the window, took aim carefully and poured it all over the already sodden book. The water carried most of the pages that weren't already fallen out away as it ran off.

The rain continued on, carrying the last straggling pieces behind. All that was left now was the cover. I figured that more water would do the trick. The binding hadn't been particularly thick or strong.

But how was I to fill the pot up more when I could barely carry it as it was? No answer came to me, so I decided to just go carefully. Maybe I'd get the strength, and maybe not, but I could still pull it.

Slowly, ever so slowly, I began dragging the water-laden pot over to the window. I could see black drag marks forming on the floor. I'd have to cover those up before Jacqueline saw them. They'd inspire too many questions.

The pump wasn't actually very far from the window, and it only took five minutes to get over while carrying my burden. It was in those five minutes that I decided that there were some questions that would never be answered. Why did water have to be so mightily heavy? This small pot had to be a thousand pounds.

It took another two minutes to hoist the water up onto the window ledge.

"And that was the end of Ian M. Wroon," I called triumphantly, pouring the water to the book below.

As expected, after the water ran off, there was nothing left of the binding. I could only hope that my excessive watering would not kill the flowers and grass around the bottom of the tower. That's the kind of thing that Jacqueline would notice.

The next few days I stayed in bed. I had no energy, and the weather wasn't helping.

The thunder and lightning were fading into the distance, but they hadn't left entirely. With the ever-present clouds, my room never got much lighter. Strong gusts of wind violently blew out all of the candles despite my most diligent efforts to keep at least one of them lit. Even my few lanterns had given up and sputtered out.

Nothing else exciting or unusual happened for the rest of the week, and I was glad. I had had enough excitement for a while.

The morning that I heard Jacqueline's familiar voice call for me to let my hair down, I almost squealed with delight, something that would have been completely uncharacteristic for me.

It was still raining, only a fine mist, but by the time Jacqueline got to the top, my hair and upper body were soaked.

She stayed all day, and we talked about nothing in particular. She didn't ask about what I had done in her absence, and I sensed that I probably should not ask about her exploits. She didn't seem to want to talk about it. Right before she left, she turned to me and grinned with anticipation.

"Tomorrow, I will not be able to stop by the tower, but I will be back the day after that. When I call for you, I am going to have a surprise."

I nodded. I could not imagine what it might be.

CHAPTER FOUR

As expected, Jacqueline showed up two days later with a large basket. It was covered with a blue and white checked cloth so I couldn't see what was inside, but that didn't stop me from trying.

"No, no, no," Jacqueline admonished me, lightly slapping my hand away and smiling to show she wasn't angry. "You don't get to see until after we eat, so sit down and finish your salad."

I sighed and settled back into my chair. I wouldn't let the subject go. "How come I get a gift? It's past my birthday."

"Aren't I allowed to give you presents whenever I feel like it?" Jacqueline asked.

I nodded grudgingly. I had hoped that she would give me a clue to what it was, but she wasn't even dropping a tiny hint. Jacqueline usually gave in to my requests, but she was getting better at saying no. I was quiet for a while. "So....the rain's finally stopped. That's something. The water will be good for the fields though. It was a dry winter," I commented before taking another bite of lettuce.

"Oh, for heaven's sakes, Rapunzel, open the gift. The day you actually become interested in the weather..." She shook her head, rolling her eyes.

I laughed. Jacqueline could see right through me. My excitement mounted as I reached for the basket and gently removed the cloth.

With a bark, something small and furry jumped out into my lap. I gasped with delight as I picked up my new puppy. It was brown with white splotches on its ears, tail, and stomach.

"Do you like him?" Jacqueline asked, eyes shining.

I picked the animal up. "He's so cute!" I pressed him to me in a gentle hug. "Does he have a name yet?"

"Not yet. That's your job," Jacqueline reached over and patted his head.

I didn't even have to think about it. "Jean Claude." I held him up to my face. "How do you like that name, my friend?"

Jean Claude barked shortly, wiggling his paws in the air. I slowly put him down and watched him scamper away, eagerly exploring. He quickly found a pot on the ground and clambered inside, whimpering once he couldn't figure out how to get out.

I laughed and picked him up, setting him back in the basket.

"Jean Claude... where did you get that name from? Your books?" Jacqueline asked.

"Yes," I said. It wasn't a lie. I did have a book with a character of that name, but I had really chosen it because that was the name of the dog I had played with at the cottage in the woods. "It's a rather good name for him, I think."

Jacqueline smiled. "Of course dear, it's lovely." She reached over and grabbed my hairbrush off of the table. "Go sit on your bed Rapunzel, your hair's getting ridiculous."

"It's fine. Don't bother," I protested lightly. Really though, I loved the feeling I got when someone else ran a brush through my hair. I sat on a pillow and started to unwind my braid.

Jacqueline sat behind me as she combed out the numerous snarls. I closed my eyes and stopped thinking for a moment. Jacqueline sang softly under her breath. She always told me that she couldn't sing, but I thought different. She said her voice was hoarse; I thought it was low and warm. It was like drinking a bowl of hot soup on a cold day.

"Jacqueline," I began. "Do you think that we'll ever to get to live a normal life?" I bit my lip. Was this the right question?

Jacqueline sighed. "I don't know. Until I get my full powers back, I can't keep you safe. But here," She gestured around the room. "Here, you will be safe."

"Yes, you're right." I guess.

Jacqueline never stopped brushing, and soon I found that my eyes were drooping. I drifted in and out of sleep. Jacqueline sang softly, not bothering to try to keep me awake. When she finished with my hair, she moved away to the kitchen. In the back of my mind, I could hear her bustling about. I was sure that she was cooking; sweet, rich scents started to drift toward where I lay on my bed.

"Rapunzel, come in, it's time to eat." I was pulled softly out of sleep by Jacqueline's musical voice.

I walked over to the table and sat down. Jacqueline set a large bowl of pasta in front of me. I brightened immediately; I had only had pasta a few times before. She sat next to me, and for the first few minutes of eating, we didn't speak. I was too busy shoveling mountains of food into my mouth and Jacqueline was content to watch me eat.

When I finished, I crossed to the window and sat on the sill, my feet hanging off of the edge. I loved to sit like this. My heart threatened to burst; I could feel my cheeks flush. Wind pulled at my hair, gently as if inviting me to go along with it, traveling the world, high above the ground.

"Rapunzel! Heavens child! You're going to be the death of me. Do be careful not to fall!" Jacqueline hovered somewhere between rushing towards me and staying away for fear of pushing me off.

A bird passed by, a streak of blue, and suddenly I remembered that I had something to tell Jacqueline.

I leapt back off of the window, ignoring Jacqueline's gasps, and flew to my closet. Throwing the doors open, I leaned in, grabbed a large jar, and made my way back to Jacqueline cautiously.

"Look! I found him on a chink next to the window. I have no idea how he got up there, but isn't he beautiful?" I held the jar up to her face. She looked closely and her expression clouded when she saw the green and yellow caterpillar inside.

"What an ugly creature," she said. My face fell, and I pulled the jar close to me, as if to protect it. Jacqueline saw my expression and smiled gently. "Well look at it my dear." She tapped the glass. "Really, you ought to throw it out."

I looked at the caterpillar; it looked back at me. *Don't hurt me,* its eyes said. I couldn't kill it now. I set the jar on a shelf, shoved in between my books. "Later," I promised. It wasn't exactly a lie. Well, it was, but it made me feel better to think that it wasn't.

The sun was setting. Jacqueline would have to leave now. We both stared out at the fading light. I sighed. I sometimes hated Jacqueline for leaving. There was enough room for the both of us in the tower. She could keep me safe here. Why would she choose to go when she could have stayed with me?

I wrapped my hair around the hook outside the window and stepped aside to let Jacqueline leave. As she stepped onto the window sill, she leaned over and kissed the top of my head. "I love you, my dear," she whispered.

"As I love you," I said.

I watched her disappear into the forest and slumped forward onto the cold stones. The heat that they gathered during the day had already leaked out. I rested my chin on my hands and stared out at the world. How I longed to go with her. Someday. Someday I would.

CHAPTER FIVE

"Rapunzel, Rapunzel, let down your hair!" The voice was unexpected. Jacqueline didn't usually come this early. It was not yet noon and I was still in bed.

Even as I jumped up, something didn't feel right. The voice hadn't quite sounded like Jacqueline's. But who else could it be? Her voice had been leaving her when she was last here; she must have caught a cold of some sort from being in the rain. That's why her voice sounded so odd, it must be.

In my hurry to get up and to the window, my foot caught on something and I fell onto my face. I looked to see what I had tripped on. It was my hair.

"Curse it all," I muttered. "Coming!" I called towards the window.

Not trusting my feet, I crawled over to the window, loosely wound my hair around the hook and let it cascade down. For a moment I rested on the floor with my back against the cool stone wall.

When I heard Jacqueline's feet hit the ledge, I stood and turned around to help her in. What I saw momentarily put me at a loss for words.

A man stood there instead of Jacqueline. I knew at once that he was the figure on the horse. We stood awkwardly for a moment in silence. He seemed to be waiting for me to speak, but I was frozen in shock.

"Um, hello there," he said nonchalantly. "Will you let me in?" He reached his hand towards me.

His words pulled me back to reality. I saw his hand and my instincts took over.

I screamed and punched him.

He lost his balance and fell backward. He seemed to have been expecting something different by the look on his face. Luckily for him, he caught my braid as he fell. It momentarily stopped him, but he could not manage to keep a hold on it. Still, it slowed his fall by a great amount. The long soft grass helped too.

I pulled up my hair as fast as I could. I was safe now.

The man sat up and looked up at me. "Now why did you do that?" he called up in dismay. "You could have killed me! It would have been horrible if I had died, don't you think?"

"I don't even know you," I replied. Stupid man.

He looked puzzled. "Yes, you do."

"Mmm... no, no, I don't."

He grinned as if it were all a joke. "Oh, come on, you are kidding, right? You remember me. I'm pretty hard to forget."

"No, really, I have never met you," I promised. "It must be someone else you are thinking of." Sure, a different maiden in a tower, in the middle of the woods. I wondered where this conversation was going.

"Come on, yes you do."

"No! I–"

He interrupted me, "Of course you do."

"I am leaving now! I hope you get bitten by a poisonous snake." I spun on my heel and stalked away from the window.

"Wait, Rapunzel, it's me, Sven!" he called.

Sven? I didn't know a Sven. I didn't even know any boys. I almost threw something at him to make him go away when I realized, I did know a boy of that name.

Visions of the village rushed at me. I ran to the window and looked down. Was it the same boy? Same dark brown hair, light eyes and skin deeply tanned as if he were always in the sun.

"Sven?" I asked in disbelief. He looked up.

"Yes, Rapunzel, we meet again." Gallantly, he swept off the hood of his cloak and bowed.

"How did you know it was me? How did you know that I was the same girl you had met?" I asked. It had been so long ago.

Sven looked at me derisively. "Really? How many girls named Rapunzel do you think are running around in the world?"

Oh. I blushed at my oversight.

"Now will you let me up?" he called when I didn't answer.

Now it was my turn to look derisive. "Are you serious? Of course not!"

"What? Why?"

"I met you once and that doesn't mean that I really know you, and as I recall, I didn't even like you when we last came into contact!"

"You don't like me? You know, I thought that we really got along! We could have been great friends if you and the witch hadn't left." He sat cross-legged, obviously resigned to the fact that he wasn't going to be getting up into the tower anytime soon

"You pulled my hair and I punched you. If that's your idea of getting along, somehow I think that your vision of things is a bit skewed."

"Ah, but…" He paused, trying to think of a smart reply. His face brightened. "See how well it worked? Here we are, repeating the exact same motions. I might add, however that your left hook has gotten considerably more impressive."

"Is that your idea of a compliment?" I asked.

"That depends. Did you like it?" My silence gave him my answer. "What if I told you that you had a beautiful voice?"

"How did you know that?" I thought. "Have you been spying on me?"

"No, of course not! I was lost and your voice called me here from the shadowy darkness I had lost myself in."

I frowned, unconvinced. "Really?"

"No. I got stuck in the storm and I have been wandering around for days. The tower was the first place I came across. I camped out in the trees while the witch was here and you sing a lot. You are quite good." He said this all very fast.

"You're still not getting up here."

"Come on! I have been in the forest with no food and limited water for what I think has been a very long time. Please let me up!"

"No. Go pick some berries or something. Someday, skills like that will come in handy," I called. "If you hold up anything you find, I'll clue you into whether or not it is poisonous. Maybe."

"If you are not going to let me up, I am going to find a way up myself!" he challenged. "It would just be easier for the both of us if you let me climb up. I just need to rest my eyes, grab some food, and then I'll get out of your hair." He laughed at his own joke.

For me, this conversation was over. I shook my head and walked away. "Do your worst, Sven," I said over my shoulder. I should not have provoked him.

I tried to go about my day as normally as possible. I read, ate, and sang lightly to myself. I did everything in my power to ignore the thought of Sven.

After about four or five hours, I couldn't wait anymore. Carefully, I crept over and peeked out the window.

"Are you going to let me up there?" Sven asked.

I frowned. He had his hands behind his head, sprawled in the grass, looking quite comfortable and mightily pleased with himself.

"No," I sputtered. "Go away."

"I'm not going anywhere. Continue on your day, if you wish. Maybe you could let your hair down for a few minutes..."

I took his advice and left again, but he would not leave my mind, whatever I did. His dark hair, his eyes, like pieces of light, both of them made my heart beat faster. The way he spoke made the hair on my arms stand up. The drawn out vowels and the way he skipped the 'h' sound made up an accent that made me smile. I had never heard anyone speak like him.

But part of me still wanted Sven to go away, to leave me alone, and that was the stronger part. Any other feelings, I strangled off.

A certain song came to mind. It had been a long time since I had heard this particular piece. One day, I had read it in a book and I begged Jacqueline to tell me the tune. I began to sing, softly at first, but my voice grew.

"Three years he fought on bloody fields
Against their Rodian king.
Scarce two and twenty summers yet
This fearless youth had seen."

At the next line, Sven's voice joined with mine.

"It was fair Mathildy that he loved
That girl with beauty rare,
And Margaret on the Ordainian throne
With her could not compare.
Long he had wooed, long she'd refused
It seemed with scorn and pride
But after all confessed her love,
Her faithful words denied."

It was an old ballad, too old to even have a name anymore which Jacqueline told me was sung as far as to the seas in the south. Still, I had not expected Sven to be well acquainted with any sort of musical literature, let alone a seldom remembered tune.

"A sad song for such a beautiful day. I have to ask you, is there a certain special young man you are waiting for?" Sven asked.

I refused to answer, but I stood still, curious to hear what he would say next.

"Giving me the silent treatment, are you? Very well, I suppose that I will just have to find out when I get up there. Prepare yourself, Rapunzel, you have never met anyone so determined, and not to mention, dashingly handsome as I!" With this he left, although not for very long.

I flopped back down upon my bed. Sven could only try to get into the tower for so long, right?

Right?

CHAPTER SIX

I stared at the spatula in my hand. It sat still, not moving.

"You and I are going to get along just fine if you would decide to finally do what I say. I'm in charge, got it?" I instructed the inanimate object.

It did not answer back.

It was three days since I had been reacquainted with Sven. I had barely gotten any sleep. In his protest to get into the tower, Sven "serenaded" me every night. Loudly. His voice was not one of his stronger aspects.

I tried dropping him food to make him go away, but he was like the wild birds that I sometimes fed crumbs. You give them something to eat once, just once, and they decided you were good for a free meal for the rest of their lives.

So I was making an omelet for the largest, peskiest bird outside my window.

"When I give this to you, you are going to finally go away, right Sven?" I called over my shoulder.

"If you make it very delicious and ask very nicely, I might just back up twenty-five feet or so. That ought to be enough, don't you think?"

"Sven, I need you to go away! I need sleep. I've been talking to my cooking supplies," I moaned, flipping the finished omelet onto a cloth napkin. I paused for a moment, looking back at the spatula. "And I think that some of them have been talking back."

"What have they been saying?"

I grimaced out the window.

"Yes, well, I could sleep a lot better if I were not in the woods, so let me up and we will both be happy!" he shot back.

He had a good point, and I considered letting him up, if only for a few hours. The thought of Jacqueline stopped me. How could I betray her like that? I couldn't bear breaking her heart. No, letting Sven into the tower was out of the question.

I stood at the window with the wrapped omelet in my hands. "Look out below," I said and tossed it down.

Sven caught it perfectly. He grinned triumphantly while I silently cursed. "Another point for me! What does that make the score? Five to three in my favor?" he called, though he knew very well that he was right.

To keep us both entertained, we had decided to count how many times Sven dropped the food I gave him. He was quite good at it. The only times he had missed was when I had deliberately thrown something at his head. I wasn't too bad an aim.

"Eat it quickly and be gone. I think that Jacqueline is coming earlier than usual today," I said.

"That, I do believe, is what you say every day, and I do not put any stock in it for one moment." He took a giant bite of my omelet.

"What will you do if she does come? She will gouge out your eyes and eat them for dinner if she finds you here."

Sven stopped eating for a moment. As tough as he talked, Jacqueline made him nervous. He hid high in a tree at night, which was when Jacqueline had inexplicably started to visit me. I wished that she would stay longer. When she was here, we could sit in silence. She would comb the end of my hair and I would doze. As soon as she left, Sven would come back out and start singing.

"She will not come. And in the meantime, I have a new plan, my most brilliant yet," Sven said, and took another bite. "This is so good. What did you put in it?" he asked, eyes closed.

"Rampion leaves," Sven gave me a blank look. "You know, rapunzel leaves," I said, grinning, satisfied that he liked it. I took great pride in my cooking.

"Mmm. Well, now I feel a bit like a cannibal. It's as if I'm symbolically eating you... well look who it is!" He turned to his left. "Jean Claude, my friend!"

I rolled my eyes. After the first day of being cooped up in my tower, Jean Claude had begun to go a bit mad—and so had I. To let him wander outside, Jacqueline had magicked a small tunnel from my room to the ground. I appreciated that, especially since I knew how hard it was for Jacqueline to use magic.

Sven appreciated it too. He had spent hours playing with him. He talked to the puppy like he was a person.

Sven whistled. "Over here, boy." Jean Claude came bounding into my view. Tail wagging, ears flopping, and tongue hanging out, he was as happy as ever to see Sven. "Hey, you. Just in time for breakfast. Oh, but you missed the cannibal discussion."

"It was not a discussion. It was a little observation you made," I corrected, trying not to smile. I was not going to be charmed by Sven.

"Jean Claude, your mistress is being grouchy. Go and make her feel better." Sven pushed the puppy away, towards the passage entrance.

Jean Claude scurried up. When he got in my sight, I knelt and scooped him up as he collided with me.

"What is your plan today?" I asked Sven. It was my customary question.

"It's a surprise." It was his customary reply.

Every day, Sven devised a new way to get into the tower. He had tried climbing a tree and jumping, scaling the wall with only his arms and legs, once he had made a ladder.

And every day, I foiled his plan. I pushed the ladder over before he could climb up, threw things at him so he would not jump, and poured water down the tower so he could not get enough of a grip on the stones.

Since he would not tell me his latest plan, there was nothing to do but wait. I sat on a chair in front of an easel and a sheet of canvas. I took up a paintbrush and studied the blank space carefully.

I wasn't near done with the picture when a loud clank made me turn around. A metal hook rested on the window sill.

In disbelief I ran over. Sure enough, tied to the hook was a rope and climbing the rope was Sven.

"This has got to be one of your most hare-brained schemes yet!" I cried in exasperation.

"Brilliant, you must mean. One of my more brilliant plans, if I say so myself," Sven grunted as he pulled himself up.

I wedged my fingers under the hook, getting ready to move it.

Sven saw what I was doing. "Wait!" he called. "Wait, don't pull it off!"

"Why not? Give me one good reason not to let you plunge to the ground. It had better be good."

"Umm... I can't think of anything. Just don't make me fall, I am bruised enough as it is."

That was true. I thought, and then grinned. "All right, stay right there." I ran over to my painting. I had just started, it was supposed to be a bird, but only the red outline had been put down and at the moment, it was rather unidentifiable.

I hauled it into Sven's view. "If you can tell me what this is, I will let you up."

Sven smiled as if this were the easiest thing in the world. "That is quite simple. It's a lobster!"

"Nope."

"Let me try again. I think that I know the trick. It's paint on a canvas!"

"Wrong again. Sorry, you're out of guesses." I pulled on the hook and slid it off the window. The game was done, with the points in my favor.

As Sven landed on the ground, I idly thought that it was a really good thing that the grass was so long and soft.

"I do have one question, Sven. Where did you manage to get your hands on a hook like that? Surely you didn't just find it lying around."

He stood, rubbing his back tenderly. "Really? I just fell fifteen feet, and all you can think to ask me about is a hunk of metal? Oh Rapunzel, you are just the sweetest person. Has anyone ever told you that?" He looked up as I awaited his answer. "All right, I found my saddlebag last night in the woods. It was in there. Satisfied?"

"Very. Now go away."

"No, I think I will hang around for a while. In fact, I feel a song coming on."

"Go, or I will set my dog on you," I threatened.

"Ha! That certainly is a good laugh."

He was right. I looked over at Jean Claude. He was as likely to attack Sven as he was to start talking.

Something else caught my eye. "I would go right now if I were you," I said, softer this time, trying to not draw attention to myself.

"That's not going to work. You can't get rid of me that easily. I've got plans to make, bruises to nurse."

"Actually Sven, Jacqueline is on her way down the hill. She will be here in a little over five minutes. I suggest that you skedaddle."

Sven paled. "Where is she?" He whipped his head around. "Which way?"

"She's far down the road. You can't see her from where you are standing. Four minutes now. Shoo." I motioned for him to leave.

Sven ran into the forest in the opposite direction I pointed to. As he disappeared into the trees, Jacqueline came into view. I had underestimated how fast she was walking. One more minute and Jacqueline would have seen Sven. As much as I loved Jacqueline and trusted her judgment in most other things, she might act without understanding the entire situation and I did not want her to hurt Sven.

"Rapunzel! Were you expecting me?" she called. "What are you looking at?"

"Nothing, I was just looking at a... lobster," I said distractedly.

"A lobster?"

"A bird, I meant a bird. Lobster, that's funny. I'm a little tired, that's all. Lobster..." I trailed off for a moment. "You don't look well. And you're in even more of a hurry than usual. Are you going to have to leave soon?"

"I have some things to do later on in the night," Jacqueline said elusively. She used the tone of voice that warned me not to inquire.

Without another word, I let my hair down for her to climb. When she reached the top, I could suddenly see the lines on the corners of her eyes. I knew that Jacqueline was far older than she looked, but I had never seen a wrinkle on her. I had never thought of her as an old woman.

"Sit down, sit down. How are you?" As always, Jacqueline was cordial and polite. Sometimes I was not sure who the guest was and who was the hostess. "You are more beautiful than ever. Perhaps it is just because I'm seeing you in the light again. It is just not the same seeing you at night."

"Why did you change the time when you came?" I asked, not sitting down. "You used to come at noon and stay until the sun set. Now you come when the sun is already gone and you leave within an hour or two.

"No reason."

"There's got to be a reason."

"Rapunzel, this is none of your business! What I do is my affair!" Jacqueline yelled.

I took a step back, stunned. My mind wandered back to the last time she had yelled at me. Both times I had stumbled across an invisible line, a line behind which lay a secret Jacqueline was never going to tell me, a secret that she seemed willing to do anything to keep me from knowing. This time however, I did not burst out into tears. I straightened my back and raised my chin.

"I am not a child anymore, Jacqueline! I have a right to ask a simple question without being yelled at. It is time that you stop treating me like I am five years old."

"Rapunzel, don't be so dramatic. When have I ever treated you like a child?" Jacqueline asked in exasperation.

I blinked, and then exploded. "You locked me inside a tower!"

"It was for your own protection," Jacqueline stuttered.

"You won't even let me cut my hair! I should be allowed to do whatever I want with it. It's mine, not yours. I think that you have a hard time remembering that."

"Oh, Rapunzel, you never would cut your hair even if I encouraged it."

I looked around, snatched a pair of scissors and held them to my braid, shaking. "What if I cut it off right now, all of it?"

Nervously Jacqueline wrestled the scissors from me. "I do not know what is wrong with you today, but I am not going to let you do anything stupid."

"It's just my hair. It can grow back," I said.

"Rapunzel, the day I let you cut your hair is the day I go against everything I believe in," Jacqueline snapped.

The angry tone of our voices sent Jean Claude barking at our heels.

"Quiet, Jean Claude, heel!" I said sharply, not even glancing his way. "Jacqueline, I think that you should leave."

"What?" She took a step back as if I had struck her.

"I don't want to talk to you anymore," I said and flung myself under the covers of my bed. I buried my face in the sheets.

Jacqueline's footsteps echoed over by the window. There was a slight scent of vanilla beans in the air. That always happened when Jacqueline performed magic. When I looked up, she was gone.

Did she really go? I thought. She'd never left like that before.

A quiet scuffling came from below. Was it Jacqueline come back to make amends? I was angry, but I wanted to be friends with her again. My list of friends was painfully short and I didn't want it to shrink anymore. What would happen to me if I was abandoned by Jacqueline?

More scuffling. I brought my head out of the bed sheets.

"Jacqueline? Is that you?" I called hopefully.

"Rapunzel, Rapunzel,

Let down your hair,

That I might climb

The golden stair."

"Ugh," I groaned. It was just Sven. "Go away!"

For once, Sven seemed to listen to me. There was no more singing. In relief I unclenched my fists and let my body relax for the first time in days.

It seemed like ten seconds later when an odd sound woke me up.

My eyes shot open, but I couldn't move. A light scratching told me that a boot had just touched the window ledge. In a blind moment of instinct, I slid farther under the blanket. Once I was completely covered, I slipped off the side of the bed and onto the cold wood floor.

In the dark, I grasped under the bed and took hold of the first thing I found. I pulled it out and felt it to discover what it was: a book. My ten pound, eight hundred page Rodian dictionary to be precise. It was one of my biggest books. Picking it up took almost all of my tired energy. Switching to a crouch, I carefully weighed the book in my hands. It was hard to keep a firm grip on it, but I would manage. I looked around. A tall, dark figure stood by my table. It just stood still, head turning side to side. I watched as the figure headed to the cupboard.

I saw my opportunity, stood, crept over to the shadow and hefted the book to my shoulder. My fingers trembled a bit. I hesitated. Could I really hit someone on the back of the head with a book? Would I really be able to hit them hard enough to knock them out?

The answer was yes. As I swung the book, the weight pulled me with it. I let it go to avoid falling over, and it clattered to the ground with a loud bang.

In satisfaction, I lit a lantern to see the intruder. In my nervous excitement, I could barely keep a grip on the handle. I held it up, and the flickering light fell on the figure's face.

I squeaked and barely managed to keep a hold on the lantern.

Sven lay crumpled on the ground.

CHAPTER SEVEN

"I'm sorry, Sven. I didn't know that it was you. If I had known, I wouldn't have hit you. Well, maybe I would have, but not as hard." I stopped and groaned in frustration. I was rehearsing what I was going to say to Sven when he regained consciousness.

He twitched and I screamed. Everything made me jump and I wasn't feeling very good. It was early enough in the morning that the stars were still easily visible. To add to my discomfort, I had put on a dress. I hadn't been able to stand near him in my nightgown. My slacks were normally my favorite attire, but I couldn't bring myself to wear them in front of Sven.

Delicately, I dragged Sven over to my sofa and left him slumped against it, dropping his tattered bag beside him.

On second thought, I picked up the black bag and pulled it onto my lap. The contents were promptly dumped onto the ground. The hook, a small telescope, a few loose papers written on in illegible handwriting, and a black piece of cloth that I could tell was covering something. I pulled back the cloth and gasped.

Out tumbled a glistening golden crown. It was just an inch tall ringlet that was covered in emeralds. I knew what that meant. I had a history book that covered the events of Ordainia for the last one hundred and fifty years. Gold crowns were for males, silver for females. Rubies were for kings and queens, sapphires for princesses and princes. The emeralds were reserved for either Crown Prince or Crown Princess, whatever the case may be.

Sven was next in line to be king.

Right at that moment, he slowly opened his eyes as if he knew that I had a question. He raised his head to see me.

"I made it in without your help," he bragged, slurring a bit, his eyes still unfocused.

"There's a large lump on your head that's getting larger by the second, and the first thing you say is how you snuck in here? You strange, strange man." I scooted closer to him, keeping the dictionary close by, just in case.

"Is that what you brought me down with?" He nodded at the book.

"Yes." I reluctantly handed it to him.

"A Rodian dictionary. I have always known that those guys had it out for me."

"What?"

"It was a Rodian witch that cursed me."

That didn't clarify anything. Why was he cursed? There were more interesting things to find out. "You might want to explain this." I held up the crown.

Sven bit his lip. "Yeah, that's a fun piece of trivia. You know, I'm a prince. That's it."

"Crown Prince, to be exact, judging by these jewels. Funny, though, that the last time I saw you, you were being kicked out of the village because no one wanted you near them," I said, swinging the crown in front of his nose.

He opened his mouth, but cut off the smart remark he was undoubtedly about to make. "Can I get some food? This is quite a long story."

"Just start talking Prince-boy," I said.

Sven took a deep breath. "After you and Jacqueline disappeared, I thought that all hopes of lifting the curse were gone. The man I traveled with was planning to get rid of me for good, I know it. So I ran away. I ended up in the capitol. Of course, with my luck, I ran in front of a horse and got kicked in the stomach. It was the king's horse and I guess he felt pity for me because he took me in. At least there was one good piece of luck in my life." He sighed heavily.

"The King is childless, and so when he got attached to you, he made you his heir," I concluded. "I thought that you said it was a long story. That didn't take so long."

"Well just for you, I skipped a bunch of the boring parts. You probably don't want to hear about all the days spent in the forest. They weren't pretty." He thought. "You seem to be quite informed about the royal family. I thought that you have been locked in a tower for six years, so how do you know any of this?"

"I read a lot, and I ask Jacqueline questions all the time." I stared at him inquisitively. "Why were you in the woods?"

"I was looking for a friend. He went missing, and I was the only one willing to look for him." He paused at my expression. "He isn't actually part of the court. He's a kitchen boy. My adoptive father didn't think it one of the duties of the king's son to be looking for him. So, of course, I set out alone."

"You are an idiot."

"Hey, he was–he is–my friend. I can't just abandon him. What would you know anyway? It's not like you ever had any friends." Sven looked regretful as soon as he said that.

"I hope that you are real proud of yourself for that one," I said coldly to Sven. He coughed awkwardly.

"Well, anyway, I went to go find him, but in the storm, my horse ran away and now I have no idea where I am."

"Wouldn't it just be grand if you could figure out which way to go and just have to pay a small favor in return?" I asked.

"I'm listening."

"I might just happen to have a certain map that would lead you to your destination." I raised my hand to stop his words. "But I don't think I would be able to find it without a promise."

"What promise?" Sven asked warily.

"You help me out of the tower. Today."

"You mean tomorrow?" Sven glanced out at the dark window.

"Yes, tomorrow. No, wait, yes, I mean." I took a breath. "It's almost morning, so I mean today. I want to leave today."

"No way, I remember what you said about Jacqueline gouging my eyes out. I don't know about you, but I want to keep my vision." Sven stood and grabbed his bag. "Help me gather my things."

I didn't move. He put every item carefully back in his bag, the crown gently wrapped in black cloth. Every item, except one.

"Where'd my telescope go?" He knelt down and started looking on the ground. "It's got to be around here…" He trailed off, looked up and saw his telescope resting neatly in my palm.

"Finally caught on have you?" I asked. "I can point you in the right direction." Not turning my back to Sven, I grabbed a roll of paper off the bookshelf. "This is a map of Ordainia. I can show you how to get wherever you want to go from here."

"What did you want again?" Sven asked, resigned.

"Let me come with you on an adventure. If we leave now, we can make it back here by nightfall," I said.

"Are you kidding? How long has it been since you've been outside?"

"Too long. I have been kept in here for too long. Please." I was reducing to begging. I shoved the map and the telescope into his hands. "I won't be any trouble. Just help me."

"Fine, but what are you going to do about your hair?" He pulled the items to himself and sat on the trunk at the end of my bed.

"My hair?"

"This stuff has got to weigh over fifty pounds!" He picked up a section of my braid that was draped over the bed. He weighed it in his hands. I yanked it out of his grasp. "You can't just let it drag behind you," he said

"I could…" Something caught my eye. "I'll just put it in this bag." I went to my bed and pulled out a travel bag that was shoved behind it.

It took a half hour to figure out how to fit my hair into the bag, and another half hour to actually wind it up and stick it in the space the bag allowed. I left the unbraided section of my hair out and swung the bag around to my back.

I packed a few bits of food into Sven's bag. He was consulting the map and looking through the telescope.

"I've got it, let's go." He turned around. "You're wearing that? A dress?"

I had on a brown traveling dress. When I thought about it, I wasn't even sure why I had one. It wasn't as if Jacqueline wanted me to go anywhere. She must have only intended on it being worn for variation or comfort.

"What do you expect me to wear?"

"Slacks, I guess." Sven shrugged.

I blushed. Wearing pants was fine when I was alone, even when I was with Jacqueline, but I wasn't comfortable enough with Sven to even think about wearing slacks without turning furiously red.

"I have leggings underneath this, I'll be fine," I stammered, walking over to the window.

The rope was still tied to the hook. I tugged on it a bit; it stretched slightly but held strong. Still, to me, it looked far too thin to hold my weight. I hesitated, my hand resting on the outside of the tower. The rising sun warmed it slowly.

"What are you waiting for? You are the one who insisted on leaving so quickly. Go on." He waved me away and folded his arms.

I lifted my skirt to my knees with one hand and steadied myself with the other hand as I stepped up onto the sill. As I turned around, I got one last look at Sven. He grinned at me, and either I was horribly mistaken or he was mightily pleased with himself.

I grabbed the rope and began to rappel down.

You're all right, you're fine. Nothing bad is going to happen, you are not going to fall, you are not going to let go, the rope won't snap, a giant bird won't come and try to carry you away, I thought.

"How're you doing?" Sven called.

"Good." My voice was shaky.

It must have been only ten minutes before I got down. It seemed like ten years.

However, it was all worth it. Once my toes hit the damp, green grass, I squeaked and let go of the rope. I wasn't wearing any shoes, I didn't have a pair. Shoes hadn't been a part of my wardrobe since I had come to the tower. Why would I have needed shoes? My feet hadn't touched real ground in six years. I couldn't hold myself up; I fluttered to the ground like a leaf. The smell of life overwhelmed me.

Sven slid down the rope. He looked at me, my nose buried in the grass. "What are you doing?

"Mmph," I muttered.

"What?"

I lifted my head. "I'm smelling the grass." I knew what he was going to say. I cut him off. "And yes, I know it's crazy." I shoved my head back in the grass.

Sven exerted a large amount of patience. He waited an entire five minutes before he nudged me up.

I stood and brushed myself off.

"Your eyes are the same color as the grass in your hair," Sven said.

"Thanks?" I said, picking the grass scraps out of my hair. I wasn't quite sure how I was expected to respond to that.

Sven continued to stare at my eyes.

I snapped my fingers and he jumped, blinking rapidly.

"You were staring at me."

He snorted in disbelief. "I was not."

"You were too, but I am not going to listen to your stammering protests. Which way are we going?"

Sven's mouth opened precisely four times. He pointed and I started off in that direction.

I couldn't stay on route for long. A bright flower caught my interest. I stopped and wandered off of our course. I delicately picked it. The rich scent overwhelmed me for a moment. It was like the grass; it smelled like life, but it was sweeter, more like a peach or an apple. After the moment, however, the flower started to fade. Disappointed, I threw it away and started walking. I wouldn't be picking any more flowers anytime soon.

Sven was remarkably patient with my delays. At least he was for the first ten times it happened.

"Rapunzel, it's just a duck. They're annoying, and they're everywhere. We'll find more, I promise. Maybe you can even keep one as a pet. Though, maybe Jean Claude would eat it. Come on, let's keep moving." It was only an hour since we had started, and Sven was already entirely annoyed with by my short attention span.

"Spoilsport," I said accusingly.

"Yes, and you have funny colored eyes. Now, are we done insulting each other? Yes? Good. Let's get a move on."

"Are you always this rude?" I asked.

"Are you always this annoying?" he retorted over his shoulder at me.

I stopped walking. Sven continued on for a few more moments before he realized that I wasn't right behind him. He turned.

"Do you mean that?" I asked, hurt.

"You know what? I do mean that. My best friend is missing, I'm stuck in the woods with a girl with hair long enough to climb and to top it all off, I have no horse!" He flung his hands in the air.

"Is that your horse?" I pointed.

A dark brown horse stood in a copse of trees off to my left. It was already saddled and it had saddlebags on its side, though one was missing. Its legs were speckled with white.

"Bruce!" Sven called and ran towards the horse. It shied away and didn't calm down until Sven slowed. "Easy boy. It's me, Bruce. Easy, easy."

The horse was wild-eyed, but he seemed to calm a little at the steady tone of Sven's voice. He let Sven touch his nose, whinnying softly.

When Bruce had completely calmed down, Sven swung up onto him in triumph, grinning broadly. He leaned over, stuck his hand into one of the saddlebags and brought out a long glistening object that I had always wished to see.

It was a sword, and it was beautiful. The hilt was golden and encrusted with emeralds. The blade was gleaming silver.

"It matches your crown," I said as Sven rode up to me.

"Yes, that it does." Sven was only paying a bit of attention to me. Most of his mind was undoubtedly concentrated on the shiny weapon in his hand.

I let him stare at it for a moment before I pulled him back into reality.

"Sven." I tugged cautiously on his pant leg. "I thought that you said that we needed to hurry."

He emerged from his trance slowly. "Oh, you're right." He sheathed his sword and held out his hand to me.

"Wait, what do I do with that?" I stared at his hand.

"You take it. I'm going to help you up onto the horse."

"Huh?"

Sven sighed. "You're going to ride the horse with me, Rapunzel. We're going to ride to the nearest town and get some real food."

"Real food?" I asked "What's wrong with my food?"

"Nothing, your food is fine, delicious even. Some of us normal people like to eat meat once in a while though." Sven's hand was still outstretched.

Meat. I hadn't had any kind of beef, chicken, or even fish the entire time I was locked up. Jacqueline didn't eat it and didn't approve of my eating it either. I couldn't remember what it tasted like.

"Rapunzel, get on the horse." Sven spoke slowly, as if talking to a child.

I hesitantly grabbed his hand. Sven lifted me up in front of him as if I weighed nothing. When his hands touched my waist, I stiffened slightly. Things like that happened so often in my books, but never to me, never for real.

As soon as I was situated, I looked around. Before, I had underestimated the height of the horse. I hadn't thought it would be a problem. Now I was scared. Quickly, I grasped the saddle.

"What's wrong?" Sven asked, laughing a little.

"I didn't think that it was going to be this high," I said shakily.

"Rapunzel, you live at the top of a tower. This isn't nearly as bad. You just climbed down that tower. Where's all that courage and stubbornness from a few moments ago?"

"This is much worse. The tower was stable, it didn't move. I couldn't fall." I took a deep breath. "Even the rope was safer. It wasn't living. It couldn't decide that it didn't like me and just throw me off. What if it decides that it doesn't like me and tries to eat me?"

Sven laughed harder and prodded Bruce with his heels. We lurched forward and my grip tightened, my knuckles turned steadily white.

As we rode, I became the smallest bit less frightened, but I was keenly aware of how close Sven was. His arms came on either side of me to hold the reins. I could hear his breathing mixed with my own. He was warm. I couldn't quite decide what I felt. Once again, I tried to squander any content thoughts.

The forest made me feel more alive. New smells and sights overwhelmed me. Colors were brighter than in the tower; birds sang louder. I remembered much of what I saw from my childhood, but the memories were fuzzy and dim while the world around me simply exploded with vibrant hues.

"How long will it take to get there?" I asked.

"Well that depends," Sven started.

"On what?"

"How fast would you like to get there?" he asked.

I suppose that I should have turned around before I answered. If I had turned around, I probably would have seen a smile on Sven's lips and amusement dancing in his eyes. As it was, I kept looking ahead when I replied, "As fast as possible, I guess."

Sven kicked Bruce into a wild gallop.

I was shoved back into Sven, barely separated from him by the bag on my back. I could almost feel his heart beating. I squeezed my eyes tight. "Sven!" I screamed. "Stop! Slow down!"

He laughed at me. That seemed to be a regular pastime of his.

We rode on, and eventually I reopened my eyes. The world rushing by was exciting to say the least. Yes, I was terrified, yes, I was livid at Sven. Something else came over me however: thrill. Bliss. There were a thousand different words I could have used and none of them could truly satisfy what I really meant.

Once I started to enjoy myself, it was all too soon before we saw the town. We slowed considerably as we got closer.

"What's it called?" I asked.

"I'm not quite sure. Perhaps there will be someone we can ask." Sven handed me the reins as we stopped.

"Don't give me those! What do I do with them?" I asked, trying to shove them back into Sven's hands.

"Hold them still. Yes, just like that. Don't pull them, perfect."

I held the reins as if they were made of glass and would break if I squeezed them too tightly.

Sven shifted his weight and began to dismount, swinging his right leg around in back.

"Wait, where are you going?" I asked. "Don't leave me alone!"

"I'm not leaving you, I'm just getting down. Do not panic," he added, slowly, making sure I caught his every word.

He hit the ground and opened the saddlebag on the left side. His hand disappeared into the brown fabric and when it came back into view, it held a long orange carrot.

I was famished. I hadn't eaten before we had left. Food had been the last thing on my mind in all of the excitement.

"Oh, thank you. How did you know?" I asked, grateful, stretching my hand out expectantly.

Sven raised an eyebrow and didn't look away as he put the carrot next to Bruce's mouth.

The horse eagerly snatched it up. For the first time, I noticed his overly large yellow teeth. Brilliant. Now I had one more reason to be afraid of the animal.

"That was mean. I'm hungry too, you know." I said.

"Perhaps so, but you are not the one who has been running at breakneck speed. If you would like to go jog in a circle for a half hour, then I'll give all of the carrots you want."

I stuck my tongue out at him, knowing that I wasn't going to win this argument.

"Give me the reins." Sven gestured with his first two fingers.

"Why?" I asked.

"I'm going to lead the horse to the town. You can't just ride in like a wild person. It's not normal for two people to not have two horses. Two people on one horse wear out the horse so much faster. This isn't a town close to anything else. To get here from most everywhere, it's quite a journey."

"But we got here easily enough."

"Yes, well, the tower is an exception. I'm pretty sure that other than Jacqueline, you, and me, nobody knows about the tower." Sven started to walk. Bruce followed him without any complaint.

"Are you sure about that?"

"About what?"

"Are you positive that no one else knows about the tower?"

Sven shook his head in disbelief. "Yes, I think that it is pretty safe to say that."

"I still don't get the reason why you're walking. Why aren't I walking?"

"Because, Rapunzel, in most societies it's custom that the men walk and the women ride the horse."

"Why? I am just as capable of walking as you are," I protested.

"I'm just trying to be chivalrous, understand? Earlier, I was not quite as polite as I was raised to be."

"Chivalry? I thought that was just a fairy tale. You really take this prince stuff seriously. I've read about it in books, but I honestly never thought that anyone acted like that," I said ponderously.

Sven turned red. "I was just trying to be nice," he muttered. "I forgot that I was talking to a girl who has practically been living under a rock."

"Oh no, it's not that I don't appreciate it, I just never assumed that a man would be so kind."

"Why not?"

"Jacqueline told me stories about men all the time, stories about how horrible and cruel they are." I could remember these tales perfectly. They were awful.

"What kind of stories? What would she tell you?" Sven asked. He sounded interested, but he didn't look at me. Perhaps it was from embarrassment.

"Uh, well." I cleared my throat. "Mostly stories of men taking advantage of young helpless girls. Her greatest fear was that I was going to meet a man and the stories would repeat themselves."

And here I was, telling this story to a man who I was alone with in the middle of the forest. I cleared my throat again.

I wanted to know if the same thought had occurred to Sven, but I didn't have the opportunity to ask. We had reached the entrance of the town. As we passed through the outer gate, goose bumps went up my arms and neck.

People were everywhere. Directly up ahead there was a large group of men and women, all standing close together.

"What are they doing?" I asked, craning my neck to try and see more clearly.

"What?" He turned. "Oh, that? It's just a market."

Apparently my books hadn't explained everything to me in enough detail to recognize everything in person.

I wanted to go closer to the market, but Sven turned the horse onto a smaller path, between two buildings.

"Wait, where are we going? I want to go over there." I tried to turn Bruce. He ignored me completely.

"To the stables. Bruce deserves a rest before we have to get you back to the tower. My plan is to not let Jacqueline even suspect that you were ever gone."

"You're right. I don't want to let Jacqueline know that I snuck out." I stopped trying to catch a glimpse of the market.

"Why don't you just leave?" Sven asked.

I frowned. "I don't want to leave Jacqueline, I love her. She's like a mother to me."

"Where is your mother?"

"Jacqueline's at her home, I suppose." I could not quite decide why this mattered. As long as she didn't find me outside the tower, what point would there be to speculate over her location?

"Do you not wonder about your real mother?"

"Jacqueline is real," I said.

"No, I mean your birth mother. What about her? Where is she now? What about your father, surely he should be around."

"I don't think that it matters much, really. I live with Jacqueline, I love her and she takes care of me. What else is there?" I asked.

"Get off the horse," Sven said. "We're ready to find Bruce a stall."

I hadn't even noticed that we had reached the stables. Now a new problem presented itself.

"How do I get down?" I looked about, trying to find a stool or something. I didn't see one, but perhaps Sven could stack a few logs on top of each other, if I could find any.

"Jump," Sven said shortly, as if it were obvious.

"Not going to happen," I informed him

"Fine, then hold your arms out." I did, and he mirrored my gesture.

I was glad that I had been riding side-saddle. Descending from the horse was enough of a leap of faith for me. Sven grabbed my waist and lifted me down. I held tightly to his forearms.

"I can't understand how you can be fine climbing a rope down from a tower, but you won't jump three feet off of a horse," he said.

"I don't trust him. I think that we already had this discussion. Horses are wild animals you know. Anything could happen," I said, brushing myself off lightly.

"Bruce is a good horse. He's very tame. He doesn't bite, squirm or buck." Sven patted Bruce's nose comfortingly.

"You're right. He only left you stranded in a thunderstorm. That's not bad at all."

"Rapunzel, there's something about horses that I don't think you understand. Enough of that." He held up his hand as I began to interrupt. "Don't think that I have forgotten about my question that you never answered, the one about your father. Let me go pay the stableman and I'll show you all around the town." He set off, leaving me and Bruce alone.

I sighed and sat down. Why didn't Sven ask me to go with him? Why did I have to stay here alone? Thoughts of that kind plagued my mind.

Because he is tired of you. He doesn't want to have to be around you any longer than he has to. The nasty voice in my head was back. I had managed to silence it ever since

Sven had appeared. Now, however, it only seemed to have gained strength. I was almost overwhelmed by sadness. Did Sven really not want to be around me any longer?

"If that's the way it is going to be, so be it. I'm going to go off alone. I'll– I'll" I stumbled for words. "I'll go have an adventure by myself." I wasn't sure who I was telling this to. Myself? No, that sounded too crazy. Bruce? That was still a little odd, but not quite as mad. "Goodbye Bruce. I'll be back soon."

I exited the stables the way Sven and I had entered. Everything appeared a little bigger than it had been when I had been on the horse. For a moment, I considered backing up and waiting, but then I looked around, took a deep breath, and walked out into the town.

CHAPTER EIGHT

"Watch it!" the man yelled as he pushed me away. I was jostled into about four other people, all of whom protested being bumped. I tried to move without disturbing anyone, but it seemed to be impossible.

"Sorry," I said for about the hundredth time.

I had a hard time navigating through the throng of people. They were everywhere: people buying and selling, people bartering, arguing and haggling. I was glad that I didn't have any money on me. From what I knew from my books, thieves reigned in places like this.

In a matter of minutes I was proven right. A man approached me. At first I thought that he was just a normal visitor to the market. As he walked by, his foot caught on mine and we both went crashing to the ground, one on top of the other.

"Oh my, I am so sorry, Miss. I don't know what happened. I have been so careless today!" the man cried, as he moved away.

"Wait a moment. Get your hand off my bag," I snapped as I started to get up. I had seen something out of the corner of my eye, and, being my paranoid self, had assumed the worst.

The man jerked his hand which had been about to open the bag still on my back.

Unexpectedly, the man smiled. "And here I took you for a naïve little girl enjoying her first trip into town."

The man stood and held his hand to me. It took me a minute to decide whether or not to take it. When I did, he helped me up.

"I guess you were wrong," I said.

"You are in luck. I am not quite in the mood to give you a fight. You don't look like you own much money." He looked me up and down. I squirmed a bit under his penetrating gaze. I didn't like something that flashed in his eyes, but it was hard to really pin down. He was, in the few moment's I'd known him, already very complicated.

"No, I suppose that I do not," I said, speaking carefully, so as to be sure of each word before it left my mouth.

What the man said next was lost on me. I couldn't take my eyes off of him. He had black hair, darker than even Sven's. It was long and ruffled, as if it had been blowing about, though there was not wind. His eyes were almost as dark as his hair. They were two deep pools of black liquid.

"I'm sorry, what did you say?"

"The name is Marius: professional pickpocket, dealer of jewelry, and when the situation calls for it, a guide to the lost, at your service." He bowed. "You are lost, are you not?"

"Yes, I suppose I could use a little direction."

"Then I would love to give my assistance, Miss..." He paused, waiting expectantly for me to offer my name.

"Rapunzel. My name is Rapunzel," I said shyly.

Marius offered his arm. "A beautiful name for a beautiful girl."

I took his arm, though somewhat reluctantly. I couldn't decide what to make of his behavior. "Where to first?" I asked.

"An inn, I should think, to get some food. Are you hungry?"

I almost cried in relief. "Yes."

We walked through the crowd together. People made way for Marius; they all seemed to know him. As we passed by, he caught the eyes of several women. He would pause briefly, excuse himself, take their hands and kiss them lightly. He was without shame in his affection, and more than one girl nearly swooned. They blamed it on the summer heat. I snorted. It was spring. Nevertheless, I still followed him through the winding alleyways that made up the town.

We were still at the inn when Sven found us. We were sitting at a table, just talking. We had finished our food, but I wasn't ready to leave the security of the building.

The door burst open and there he was. He seemed to take up the entire door frame. As soon as he caught sight of me, his entire gaze darkened.

"Rapunzel." His voice wasn't very loud, indeed, I was surprised that I could hear it at all, but the stern tone it carried over to me, was worse than if he had yelled.

I wanted to hide, but I had the suspicion that there was no getting away from the fact that I had left him without a word as to where I was going. I was his responsibility, and I had no doubt that he took that seriously. I ran my fingers through my hair. I had meant to try and find him eventually,

I really had, but it had slipped my mind. Indeed, I had almost forgotten how I had come to be in town at all.

He strode over to our table and looked at me for an endless moment. "I get out of the stable, and you've disappeared. At first, I think that perhaps I had told you wait somewhere else, but no. I'm sure I didn't. Why would you think it a good idea to wander off by yourself?"

"I'm not stupid, Sven. I can find my way without you," I shot back angrily, my initial embarrassment wearing off to be replaced by indignation.

Marius stood. "Is this man bothering you, Rapunzel?"

Sven ignored Marius. "What about Jacqueline? How dumb do you think she is? All I can think of is her carving out my eyes. I like my vision, Rapunzel. I can't really afford to lose it." He grabbed my elbow and started to pull me towards the exit.

I tried to hold my ground, but Sven was far too strong for me to resist. I had to follow him to avoid falling over. His grip was cutting off the circulation in my arm.

"Ouch, Sven, let go," I protested.

"You heard her, let go." Marius put his palm warningly on Sven's shoulder.

Sven drew his sword and pointed it at Marius who backed up in surprise. I wearily covered my eyes with my free hand. This was getting quickly out of hand.

"Do not touch me." Sven held the sword stationary until Marius held up his hands in resignation and sat back down.

"We're going, Rapunzel," Sven said firmly.

"Fine, I'll come. Next time though, if Jacqueline gets you, it's not my problem." I jerked my arm out of his hold and looked back.

"Goodbye. Thank you for helping me, Marius."

"Will you be back?" he asked.

"Yes," I said.

"Definitely not," Sven said at the same time.

Marius smiled and winked at me.

"Bruce is outside for you. Go wait for me." Sven pushed me behind him.

I strutted away from Sven and Marius. Bruce looked more refreshed than he had before. At least one of us wasn't emotionally drained.

I was not sure quite how to mount the horse, so I just leaned up against him. As he took huge breaths in and out, his side moved up and down, the sensation calming.

People passed me by, many without even having looked at me. One little girl, however, kept walking past, back and forth. She looked at me out of the corner of her eye.

I tried to see if Sven was coming back. I couldn't see him, but I did see something else that was interesting. The little girl was standing on tiptoe, whispering to a man, her hands circling his ear. After she was done speaking, the man handed her a shiny coin and she melted into the surrounding crowd of people.

The man straightened and headed towards me. He had on a long brown coat, but looked unarmed. "Well, good day, Miss," he said. "I couldn't help noticing you, looking so beautiful and alone. And with such long beautiful hair too." He grinned, and it sent shivers down my spine.

"Thank you," I whispered, unable to make my voice rise any more.

"Why don't you come down to the tavern with me and a few of my..." He paused. "Friends."

"No, thank you. I don't think I will." I tried to take a step back, but Bruce's warm body blocked me.

"Oh, come one, dearie. It will be lots of fun." The man stepped too close.

"No. Leave me alone." I started to head back towards the inn; suddenly I wasn't so mad at Sven. I wanted someone who could use a sword near me.

The man grabbed my waist and yanked me to him. I tried to scream, but the man gripped my mouth with a grim covered hand. His breath was hot and wet. I wanted to gag at the smell of it. A panic started to creep over me, but I thought that I knew what to do. With all of the courage I could muster, I bit into the man's finger as hard as possible. Blood filled my mouth. I hadn't expected that. I spat, repulsed by the warm liquid.

"Ow! Woman!" He raised his bloody hand to strike me.

I squeezed my eyes shut and waited for the sting.

It never came.

I opened my eyes and saw the man flinching away. A sword pressed itself to his throat. Holding the sword was Sven.

"Let her go." Sven's voice was quiet, but it rang in my ears as loud and pointed as a trumpet.

The man released me with one final squeeze and backed away, hands held up in the air. He did not look quite as scary anymore.

"Walk away. Don't come back," Sven hissed. The man ran, glancing back carefully, making sure that Sven wasn't behind him. "If I have to pull my sword out one more time today for you, girl, I'm going to board up that tower for good." He sheathed it and angrily lifted me onto the horse.

As he mounted, I caught sight of the little child I had seen before, standing directly to the side of Bruce.

"Sir," she said in a thin voice. "Sir, you never gave me my coin." She held out her hand.

Sven flipped a copper coin to her. She caught it and scurried away.

"Wait, I've seen her before," I said. I craned to try and see her better. She disappeared even as I looked.

"She's a snitch. She makes her money from selling information. She told me that you were in trouble." Sven whipped the reins and Bruce started to walk.

"What a strange thing for a little girl to do. Are there many like her?"

"Yes. Only the smartest end up like that, the ones who realize that they could make a little money. For her there were two choices: beg or snitch."

I was bothered by this. My tower was filled with everything I could ever want. The idea that small children had to work to survive puzzled me.

We were silent for a while after that. It was an uncomfortable silence, and I figured that I was going to have to be the one to break it.

"I hope you understand, you had no right to tell me what I can and cannot do," I said. "You are not in charge of me."

"As your friend," he started, "I have the responsibility to make sure—"

I spun around where I sat. "You don't have any responsibility concerning me. I'm not sure that we're friends, Sven."

"Why wouldn't we be friends?" Sven looked puzzled.

"What do you think? Number one: I don't care what you say; we only really met a few days ago. Two: even talking to you goes against everything that I've ever been taught. Three: the only reason you even brought me along is because I blackmailed you into it." I turned back around and held tight to the saddle.

Sven didn't speak, at least for a while. "Rapunzel, I–" He lost his thought. "I did not mean to offend you," he said slowly. "I was just, I was only..." He gave up.

I didn't justify that pathetic attempt on an apology with words.

We reached the tower just before the sun set. This time, I jumped off the horse by myself even though it made my breath catch in my throat. I didn't want Sven's help.

The rope was still there. I breathed a sigh of relief that I hadn't realized I had been holding. I had secretly been worried that it would be cut or fall or somehow be gone. That would have left me stuck at the base of my home.

Jean Claude was still there too. He barked incessantly at the sight of us. When he saw Bruce, he leaned forward on his front paws and started to growl, showing his teeth in what he must have thought was a menacing expression.

"Jean Claude! Be quiet!" I instructed.

He calmed down, but only after I scooped him up and scratched him behind the ears.

"Shoo, Jean Claude; go back to the top of the tower." I set him down and nudged him in the right direction.

As always, Jean Claude completely ignored what I told him. He started towards Sven, who had also gotten off the horse.

"Jean Claude, get away from him," I said.

The stupid dog just whined at me and sidled up to Sven's leg.

"Hey, you. Good boy." Sven leaned down and patted Jean Claude's head. The puppy wagged his tail and jumped up to put his paws on Sven's legs.

"Traitor," I muttered.

Jean Claude barked and panted contentedly. At least he was happy in his disloyalty.

"Fine, Jean Claude, stay here. I don't care." I walked over to the rope. As I grabbed it, something occurred to me. Climbing down the rope had been hard, but not impossible. Reversing the process was going to be considerably more difficult. I hesitated. I definitely did not have the arm strength to get up. In fact, I wasn't even sure how I had made it down.

"Figured it out sweetheart?" Sven asked, leaning casually against Bruce and eating an apple.

I hated that he could be so soft and fragile when he was apologizing, but an hour or two later, he was as sarcastic as ever.

"Listen, you're not going to get anywhere by yourself. Why don't you swallow your pride and we can work this out together," he continued when I kept my mouth shut.

"And just what do you suggest?" I asked, a little sick of his surly attitude.

Sven pulled a second rope out of the saddlebag. Walking forward, he ran the rope through his fingers, staring upward, looking questioningly at the window and the hook that held the first rope.

"I'm just going to have to do this a tad differently than before." He was muttering to himself, not to me.

"How did you do this the first time?" I asked. The question had been on the tip of my tongue for a while.

"I tied a loop in the rope and threw it until it caught on the hook," he said, distracted.

I wanted to ask why it was so important for him to get into the tower that he would work that hard, but somehow I knew that this wasn't the time to ask. "Is that what you're going to do?"

"No, didn't you listen? I need a way to pull you up. I'm going to throw the rope over the hook and we'll go from there."

I watched as Sven backed up, studying the rope intently. He drew his arm back and launched the rope. The coil flew through the air. It went rather high, but the window was so far away that I didn't think that there was any chance it was going to clear the hook. To my astonishment, it did.

"Yes!" Sven began to feed the rope over the hook until each end lay on the ground. He started to tie a loop into the end, but stopped suddenly. "Would you rather climb up by yourself, or be hoisted up to the window?"

I thought. Climbing would be harder, but being pulled up by Sven would be humiliating. And really, when was I going to get to do something more exciting than climb up the wall of what had been my home for six years? I had always imagined doing something like this, so I thought that I might as well make it a reality.

"Climb," I said.

"All right, I need to tie this around you." Sven stepped forward, the tough, angry man gone, leaving a timid boy in front of me.

He pulled the rope around my torso in an 'x' pattern. Once he had repeated the knot twice, he tested it, gingerly tugging it, and then stepped back.

"This isn't going to be the most comfortable way, or even the safest way, but it will work. Anyway, the goal is to not fall, so as long as you don't fall, you'll be fine." Sven tightened each of the knots.

That was not exactly reassuring.

"Thanks Sven, I'll remember that. Don't fall, or I'll be in a lot of pain. But what if the ropes snap?"

"Actually, the rope won't snap. Most likely, it'll just slip off you. Of course, that's only if you fall at all. Which you won't. Probably."

"You're really motivating. I feel much better now."

"Good. It's time for you to start climbing."

Deep breath. It didn't really help. I took a deeper breath. "Do I just go whenever I'm ready? I mean, do I wait for you, or can I just wait until I'm completely sure that I won't topple?"

"Just go. Preferably sooner rather than later. You climb, I'll pull up the slack so that if needed, I can keep you suspended." Sven braced himself with the rope. "But if at all possible, don't fall."

I was beginning to hyperventilate. I took another deep breath. "Here I go."

As I put my hands on the first stones, I noticed that my fingers were trembling, and not just a little. I ignored that, or I tried to. I had to convince myself that I was not afraid or I was never going to make myself move.

"Are you sure that this is possible?" I asked.

"Positive. There are plenty of handholds all of the way up. Stop worrying and get up there." He tugged empathetically on the rope, making me jerk a little.

I did what he said and started up the tower. My fingers grasped at the chinks in the cold stone with a fierceness I had never known I had.

"Rapunzel! Position your feet higher up! More, more, good, now you can push your body up with your legs rather than having to pull it up with your arms alone."

I tried this, and suddenly climbing was ten times easier. I was eternally grateful that I never wore a dress without wearing leggings. At least I didn't have to worry about Sven seeing up my skirts. And it was probably a good thing that I didn't have shoes. My bare feet let me stick my toes in between the stones.

About halfway up, I glanced down. Bad idea. I had read a million times that the worst thing to do was look down when high in the air, but I had underestimated how tempting it would be. Sven was tiny, Bruce was small, Jean Claude a mere pinprick. I wished that I didn't have such good vision. Then perhaps I would've realized how high I was with such dizzying clarity.

Oh my. Oh my," I breathed. My vision swam. I felt as if I were trying to look through syrup.

Sven must have seen my terror, for he yelled, "Rapunzel, it's all right. You'll be fine! Look in front of you. Think about being in the tower, safe."

"I can't do this!" I yelled back.

"If you don't toughen up and climb, I'm going to cut off every yellow inch of that insanely long hair!" Sven threatened.

I silently laughed. Not for one minute did I believe that Sven would go through with that, but it boosted my confidence.

When I felt the windowsill with my fingertips, relief washed over me. I had done it. It was over. I hauled myself over the ledge and lay on the floor, exhausted. Eventually, I stood up and looked down at Sven. "You'd better go. This took a longer time then perhaps it should have. Jacqueline will be here soon."

Sven nodded and got onto Bruce. As he started to leave, I panicked.

"Come back tomorrow?" It was a question. I was not confident that he would agree with me and come back, and I didn't feel comfortable enough to tell him outright that I wanted him to do so.

Sven thought. "Yes. I will come." And then he was gone.

"Jean Claude." I whistled and the puppy disappeared into his tunnel.

The ropes were pulled inside the tower. The last thing I needed was Jacqueline thinking that something was wrong, and so they were coiled and stuffed underneath my bed. I was just in time, too. A voice came from below the tower.

"Rapunzel!" Jacqueline was back.

I suddenly remembered that my hair was still in the bag on my back. I opened it, pulled my hair out and let it unravel. The bag was thrown to the ground.

I dropped my hair with a sigh. I knew that people were not supposed to be able to feel their hair, but I always felt awkward when it was wrapped up.

I saw Jacqueline's face and her expression. They weren't very encouraging.

"Rapunzel, I was worried that you weren't going to let me up." She stepped over the sill.

"Why?" I asked, not bothering to pull my hair up. I was counting on this being a brief visit, hoping that she wouldn't stay too long.

"You were so upset when I left, I wasn't sure if one day was enough for you to recover."

One day? It felt like a week had passed.

"I'm sorry, Jacqueline, I didn't mean to attack you the way I did."

"Oh darling, it's perfectly all right." Jacqueline never could stay mad at me, no matter what happened.

I was glad that we could be done fighting. I loved Jacqueline so much. When we were having a fight, life was miserable. Nothing was fun when we weren't talking. Not only did I lose my only friend, but when she was angry, she would stay away until she had calmed down. Sometimes that would be days, and when she didn't come back, I didn't get more food.

"I have to ask. Do you really want to cut your hair off?" Jacqueline stared unblinkingly at me after she asked this.

I thought. No, I didn't. I loved my hair. It was part of who I was. I shook my head. "I could never really cut it. I was angry, so I said something I thought would hurt you."

"I feel much better now that's out of the way, don't you?" Jacqueline stood. "I have things to do, places to be. I will be back again tomorrow, darling." She came over to the window and climbed over the sill.

"Wait!" I said hurriedly. Jacqueline raised her eyebrows, but hesitated. "The other night, did you magic yourself out of the tower?"

Jacqueline smiled mischievously. "Yes, I do have a few tricks up my sleeve, even if my magic isn't all it used to be." She slid down to the ground and I brought my hair back up.

I slipped my nightgown on and climbed into bed. It was warm and safe under there.

Images floated through my mind. Some bad: riding the horse. Others were good: the forest and the colors that made it up.

I smiled when I thought of the flowers. Though I had thrown away the first one I picked, later, I had grabbed a bright orange lily growing by a small pond right near the tower. This one hadn't wilted yet. I placed it behind my ear, but it got squished by my hair, so I pulled out and placed it in a vase. Jacqueline had never brought me flowers. Maybe she hadn't wanted me to have any reminder of the world.

Contrasting thoughts of Sven and Marius swam in my mind. I couldn't stop thinking about them. But really, did I know either of them? No, I didn't, but I wanted to. It was confusing.

I closed my eyes and tried to stop the thoughts from invading my mind.

CHAPTER NINE

I woke early and bounded out of bed. "Good morning world," I trilled as I bounced over to the window. I leaned out and closed my eyes, feeling the cool air on my face.

I hadn't been this happy in a long time. Today, I was going to see Sven, get out of the tower and see the world. What more was there to ask for?

Jacqueline had secretly left me food. Wheat rolls stuffed with seeds and cheese; fruit, mainly oranges and pears; all sorts of things. I ate an orange quickly. The rest I would save for later in the day.

I didn't have the patience to wait for Sven and I set to the arduous task on fitting my hair in the bag all alone. In the sparse extra room in the filled bag went as much food as would stay without falling out. It was a challenge to latch, but I figured that it would be well worth it.

The rope tumbled down the tower just as my hair did every time Jacqueline came. If the rope had been golden and knotted, the two would look exactly alike, excepting of course, that my hair was attached to my head and the rope was not.

I attempted to slide down as Jacqueline had pulled off so nicely, but I did not have the talent for that. About three quarters down, the rope felt very slippery. I fell and hit the ground hard.

"Oof," I muttered. Now I knew how Sven felt. I had only fallen once and it hurt. He had hit the earth twice and only complained a few times. I was going to be complaining about my bruises all day long.

I pushed the few loose strays of hair out of my face and stood, surveying the scenery. The morning was still new. Mist crept along the grass sneakily, leaving dew in its wake. The moisture chilled my feet, but I liked the way the plants pushed in between my toes.

I knew Sven would not be here for quite some time. The sun was still just a rumor, and several stars were visible. It wasn't really morning yet, but I couldn't wait for another chance to explore.

"Jean Claude!" I called. He probably wasn't awake. The dog's energy knew no bounds during the daytime, but in the early morning, he was about as active as a slug.

The sounds of a small animal shuffling echoed down the tunnel. Jean Claude emerged, ears drooping, eyes halfway closed. He walked haphazardly, in danger of running into a tree.

I pulled out a pear and Jean Claude's entire countenance changed. The puppy had a strange love for the fruit. His ears perked and his tail went wild. I threw the pear and Jean Claude ran off madly in search of it. When he returned, he held the pear proudly in his jaws. He strutted around in a circle, holding his prize high in the air.

"Oh, very good, Jean Claude. You think that you are so clever, now don't you?" I said, tickling him under his chin as he passed in front of me.

Jean Claude barked his agreement happily, but in doing so, he lost his hold on the pear. He snatched it back up quickly and glanced at me bashfully. It was not the first time he had done that. He forgot that he could not bark and hold something in his mouth at the same time.

"Nice work, Jean Claude," I said. "Just eat the fruit; you'll embarrass yourself if you keep this up."

I lay on my stomach in the grass, picking out the small strands one by one.

"You know that you can make a whistle with that, don't you?" A quiet voice asked, creeping out of the forest like the morning mist.

I jumped and got to my feet, but I didn't turn around. I still clutched some grass in my fists.

"Is that so? I've never tried that," I answered.

"Hmm, funny, I would have judged you to be the type who had seen it all and done it all." The voice was closer. "I guess that I'm not as good of a judge of character as I thought I was."

Sven pulled the grass out of my hands. I turned and watched as he put two pieces of the plucked grass together and placed them on his lips. As he blew, a high buzzing sound whistled. For a few seconds, it was the same note, but Sven soon started to pick out a simple tune. I recognized it as one of the dancing songs from the village. It wasn't quite the same as I remembered, but it still made me laugh. It was a song about the girl who loved a goat.

"It's not the most beautiful sound, and it's sometimes extremely painful on the ears, but I grew up making these, and I suppose that I never stopped." He handed the makeshift instrument to me.

"How long have you been standing there?" I asked, rubbing the grass between the tips of my first and second fingers.

"Long enough to realize that you were never going to look up unless I said something." He laughed. "And really, I didn't want to stand still until you picked out all of the grass around you."

"But just think: if you had waited, there would have been enough grass to make a few thousand whistles." I experimentally blew on the grass. No noise came out.

"Squeeze your lips together," Sven advised.

"Like this?" No sound.

"No, more." He got two more pieces and demonstrated. The instrument whistled a small series of notes, low to high.

"This?" A pathetic wheezing sound oozed out of the grass pieces.

"Obviously not. Here, let me help." He pushed my hands down and placed his fingers on the top and bottom of my lips. "Just like this." He pushed his fingers together, squeezing my lips into an absurd position. "See? Got it now?"

I nodded, trying desperately not to giggle.

"Sorry, I couldn't hear you." He squeezed tighter.

"Mph." I batted his hands away, laughing. "I think I've got it." This time when I blew on the grass, it sounded about the same as when Sven played it. I grinned. "I did it! Did you hear that?" I blew once more. "I did it again!"

"That's good, for an amateur anyway. There is no chance that you're ever going to be as skilled as me."

I shoved him playfully with my shoulder. "Thanks for showing me this." I spun the whistle in my hand.

"Does this mean we're friends?" Sven asked, with one eyebrow raised.

"On one condition." I folded my arms. I had been thinking for a while. Sven might be able to teach me how to use a sword, a real sword, just like his. In storybooks, it was always helpful if the characters could swing something heavy around to fight evil with.

"Oh? And what it that?" Sven mirrored my stance.

"You are going to teach me to sword fight."

"Sword fight," he repeated.

"Sword fight, shoot an arrow, throw a knife, use a sling. I'm sure that you could think of something. All I want is to be able to defend myself. You can't very well expect me to depend on you if I'm in trouble."

"May I ask why?" Sven looked very skeptical. There was a hint of a smile on his lips, as if he were fighting back laughter. He didn't think so, but I was deadly serious.

"The man in Acada. If something like that happens again, I need to be able to protect myself. I am not going to count on you being there to save me all of the time."

"What man?"

"The one you pulled your sword on yesterday."

"I pulled my sword twice. You are going to have to be a bit more specific. Which incidence are you referring to? The man on the street, or the thief you willingly had lunch with?"

"Stop making fun of me."

"Fine. I know what you're talking about, but I think that you are being crazy." Sven shredded the grass in his fingers. "Women don't need to learn to fight."

I stepped forward until my face was only a few inches from his. "I'll have you know that I have more courage and will than many men." I glared at him, seething in anger. "Let me rephrase this so that you can understand: teach me, or I'll tell Jacqueline about you. How much do you want to keep your eyes in their sockets?"

Sven just smirked. "You have really got blackmailing down to an art." He stepped even closer. "I'll do it." I had to look up to see into his eyes. Sven continued on, "Though, in reality, you'll probably just poke out my eye with an arrow." He batted the grass remains out of my grasp and started to move away. "Today, however, you'll be learning to ride."

"Wait, ride what?" All the confidence I had briefly felt disappeared.

"A horse, Rapunzel, you are going to ride a horse." He stood back and I caught sight of Bruce and a second horse, reins tied to his saddle. It was white with a few roan splotches. "What do you think? She's beautiful, isn't she?" He jogged over to the horse and petted her nose.

"She? What's her name?" I asked.

"Not sure. I suppose that means that you get to choose. What do you think her name should be?" Sven pulled me over to pet her.

"Resa," I said immediately. Resa was the name of the heroine in one of my favorite books. Her story ended up with a happily ever after, but not a prince, making it an exception in my collection, when so many other women always ended up with a man to save her.

"There you have it. Resa it is. Here, feed her some carrots. Make her your friend." He stuffed a few carrots into my hand.

"Hi, Resa. Sven says that we're going to be friends and I figure that we better listen to him seeing as he is Crown Prince and all. He could have us both executed for looking at him the wrong way, you know." I watched as Resa gobbled the vegetables out of my hand, carefully making sure that her large teeth didn't come too close to biting off my fingers.

"Funny how you only remember that little fact when it serves you a good purpose. Shouldn't you do what I say all of the time?" Sven asked.

"Sorry, selective memory. It's such a curse. I bet it runs in my family, but of course, I wouldn't know. So, what happens now?"

"First step is to get on the horse. Step over by the stirrups, good, right there. Now, grab the saddle horn, no, not that." He pointed out the correct spot. "Are you holding it tightly? Now, put your right foot in the stirrup. That's good, just stand up on your right foot now. Make sure you keep a firm grip on the saddle."

I wobbled dangerously, but I was doing it. I was going to ride a horse by myself! Resa stirred and I squealed, holding tight to the saddle.

"Why couldn't I have just learned to fight?" I asked. As quickly as the excitement had come, it drained out of me, leaving me once again scared to death of the animal.

"For that I will need to get another sword and a bow. Now stop worrying, you'll be fine. You should be concentrating on the task at hand."

"I am!"

"Are you sure? If you aren't concentrating properly, you're likely to be thrown from the horse and trampled by her hooves," he said.

"Sven! Don't say that!"

He chuckled a bit. "Swing your left leg around the back of the horse and you'll be set to ride." Sven swung casually onto Bruce.

"I'm not going to be riding side-saddle? I can't ride like a man." I wobbled some more. This was a difficult position to maintain.

"Why not? Side-saddle is only convenient when I have to lift you onto the horse, and not really even then. Otherwise it is terribly impractical. You can ride any way that you want, it doesn't honestly matter, but keep in mind that there will be no one to see you, so you need not worry about propriety."

Blushing furiously, I did as he said. To my surprise, I found that I preferred this method to the lady-like way. It felt more secure. I was no longer convinced that I was going to fall off. I had to adjust my skirts a few times to get comfortable, but it was worth the trouble. It would take a lot more to get me to fall when riding like this. There was still fear nagging me in the back of my mind, but I was no longer overwhelmed by the thought of being thrown off.

"Is that so bad?" Sven asked. I shook my head. "I hate to say that I told you so," he said. What a rotten liar.

"Then don't. What do we do next?" I asked expectantly.

"Grab the reins. No, not like that! Gently, gently, good. Resa will respond to prompts from both your toes and the reins. When you wish her to move faster, tap her sides with your heels. Make sure not to stab her, a soft nudge will be all she needs. To turn, pull gently on the reins in the direction you want her to go." He shifted restlessly, as did Bruce and Resa, all three of them obviously ready to ride. "Stay away from anything you would need to jump over. I don't need you killing your horse as a result of some crazy idea that you're going to be good at this."

"All right, I think that I got it all. Be gentle; try not to jump too high." I tightened my grip on the reins. "Let's go." I nudged Resa with my toes.

"Be careful," Sven added quickly, but calmly.

Too late. Resa reared and I slipped off of her back, landing painfully on my bottom. Resa pranced forward a few stops and stopped to graze.

"What did I tell you? Maybe if you would learn to listen to others, you wouldn't get in so much trouble."

"Just shut it." I stood, trying to hold together my last bits of dignity and ignore Sven's chuckles. "Well, goes to show that I'm no good with horses. They just hate me. That means that it is time to go back to the fighting idea, right?"

"No," Sven started carefully. "This just goes to show that you're going to have to be very resilient to pull this off."

"You want me to get back on? Are you crazy? You saw what just happened." I glared at him. "You really want me dead, don't you?"

"Oh I saw. In fact, that was so amusing that I would not mind if you fell again. And I don't want you dead. Perhaps just as bruised as I am, maybe even a little scratched up, but not dead." Sven walked Bruce over to where I was. "Get back on Resa."

"I am not going anywhere near that wild animal."

"Wild animal? Resa is the tamest horse that I could find who was fit to ride. Come on Rapunzel, don't be scared. You probably won't fall off again."

"I'm not scared, Sven. My common sense just speaks louder than my sense of idiocy. You remember common sense don't you?"

"Common Sense? Yes, I remember that, but only vaguely. I kicked it out of my head a few years ago. It wouldn't stop clashing with my instincts and one of them had to go."

I slowly got back up on Resa. "You ever think that perhaps it was just clashing with the curse? Natural feelings against witchcraft, you're bound to lose all bits of sanity."

"Ahh, the curse. See, there's a funny thing about the curse. In the village, they kicked me out because they were afraid of the curse, and I always thought that they were in the right to do so. I was a disaster waiting to happen. Now that I think about it, I realized that it was all part of the curse itself. It wouldn't matter if it went away. No one would ever take me in. I have accursedly bad luck." He shook his head. "And now that you have managed to wrangle out my deepest darkest thoughts, it will soon be my turn to embarrass you, but not yet. Are you ready now?"

"You call that deep and dark? Hardly. Anyone could tell that you have rotten luck simply by looking at you. Then again, maybe that's as deep of a thought as you can form." I stopped. "Ready for what?"

"Just answer yes or no," Sven said. There was something mischievous in his eyes that I didn't like.

I pressed him into answering my question. "Ready for what, exactly?"

Sven sighed. "Are you ready to go?"

I bit my lip. "No, definitely not."

"Excellent." He whistled. "Come on Resa, let's go. Rapunzel, make her start."

I tapped her sides gently. "She won't–" I gasped as Resa started to run. "Make her stop, make her stop, make her stop!" I pulled back on the reins frantically.

Resa halted and I jerked forward.

"Never do that again." I put my hand to my neck. It throbbed a bit, but I wasn't going to let Sven know that.

"That was good, but this time, try not to stop so suddenly. It's less painful when you take it slowly."

"You are really not going to let me get off, are you?"

"Nope. You are going to ride this horse if it kills you." Sven was only barely suppressing a smile. I could see it playing at the corners of his mouth. He seemed to always be ready to laugh.

"It is going to kill me."

"As long as you accept your fate. This time, flick the reins a little before you dig your heels in. She's a good horse, but she gets spooked if you don't give her fair warning." Sven guided Bruce to stand by Resa.

"You could have said that to me before," I muttered.

"I tried, but not very hard, I'll admit. It was so much more fun to let you try it for yourself. You won't be so cocky this time, I think."

"I'm never cocky," I protested.

"If you say so. Let's see if you can manage to stay on the horse once more." He flicked his own horse's reins and started off at a brisk walk.

Cautiously I did the same. I bit my tongue when Resa took the first step. She walked faster than I was comfortable with at first, but as soon as she had caught up with Bruce, her pace leveled out.

"See? Not quite as terrifying as you thought." Sven kept his gaze ahead, but I couldn't resist turning to glance at him, afraid as I was of falling off.

"No, not quite," I said, my voice only a little shaky.

"Good. Since that is the case, and because we are clearly not quite friends, I am about to teach you a lesson in speed." Sven reached into his pocket.

"What does that mean?" I asked, not suspecting what Sven had in mind.

Sven brought out a whistle. It was very thin, long and made of wood. A real whistle, not a pretend one like the whistles he made out of grass. He winked at me. "Good luck." He blew on the whistle.

What had been a light, brisk walk transformed into a frantic chase.

"Stop, stop, stop!" My voice elevated in pitch. "Sven, make her stop! I am going to fall. I'm going to fall and then I'm going to die!"

Out of the corner of my eye, I spotted Sven and Bruce gaining on us rapidly. I calmed a little, sure that help was on the way. When Sven reached me, however, I saw the wide grin pasted on his face and I knew that he wasn't coming to help me.

"Sven, make her stop!"

"Are you kidding? I knew that there was no other way to get you running. Resa won't stop until I blow the whistle a second time. Come on, have a little fun. Let's race!" Sven leaned forward, concentration flooding his face. I tried to copy him, as I leaned forward in a similar fashion, but I simply fell further and further behind.

It was a fortunate thing that Resa could steer herself because there was no chance I would be able to navigate through all of the trees.

I had not known that riding a horse could possible take so much energy. Soon there was sweat dripping down my forehead and back. Finally, Sven slowed and Bruce reared, protesting the abrupt change in speed. He blew the whistle, prompting Resa to slow and stop.

"Ha-ha! I do believe that I win." Sven didn't come back to where Resa had stopped to graze, but rather made me catch up to him.

"That was the most idiotic thing I have ever participated in," I panted, trying to keep a hold on my breakfast.

Sven swung off his horse and landed gleefully on his feet. "Bow to the winner. You may bask in my glow, if you wish." He strutted around a few times.

I could not answer. My breathing quickened more and more until it seemed I wasn't breathing at all. Air seemed to have gotten trapped somewhere in between my mouth and my lungs. In desperation, I put a hand to my throat, panic rising.

"Rapunzel, are you all right?" Sven asked, coming closer, the triumph around his eyes fading a little.

A few squeaks escaped my mouth. Air started to flow, but not nearly enough. I lost my grip on the reins and felt myself slip sideways off of Resa. I hit the ground but I couldn't even pay any care to the pain. Dots black as night started to fill my vision.

"Rapunzel, Rapunzel! Answer me!" Sven rushed over and knelt next to me.

Air, I tried to say. *I can't get enough air.*

More black dots invaded my vision. They scared me and I closed my eyes so that they would go away.

"Rapunzel, Rapunzel!" Sven must have been shaking me because I could feel ground bumping against my back.

Go away, I thought.

His voice stopped.

My eyelids felt so heavy, as if they were weighed down with large metal plates. I struggled to open them. Eventually, slivers of light appeared. That was encouraging.

"Rapunzel, are you still here? Say something." The voice confused me. It was a man's voice, but not Sven's. I had been expecting Sven's voice. We were alone in the forest, who else could it be?

"Look, she's fine now. You can leave." That was Sven's voice.

"Get your hands off of me. I have as much right to be here as you do," the voice said angrily.

A bell went off in my head. I knew to whom the voice belonged.

"Marius?" I asked softly, still working on opening my eyes. They felt sewed shut.

"See? She said my name. She wants me here. Go away." There was a pressure next to me, like someone had sat nearby.

"I was the one who got her here, I'm not going anywhere. If you have a problem with me, you can leave. No one is going to try and stop you"

My eyes finally decided to cooperate. They snapped open. Marius' dark eyes watched me, concerned. Though I had recognized his voice, I was still surprised. That was one of the last things I had been expecting. Marius hadn't been in the woods, so where was I? I lifted my head a bit to see. I was on a hard bed in a small room. The room was painted black, an odd color for a bedroom. There were a few large windows on the wall across from me; the light impeded by heavy, ash-colored curtains. A desk the size of a horse lurked in a corner, stark white against the dark walls.

"What am I doing here? Where am I?" I sat up slowly, ignoring the throbbing in my lungs.

"The town we went to yesterday, Acada." Sven stood in a back corner, arms crossed, leaning sulkily against the wall, obviously not happy about Marius' presence.

"Sven brought you here a few hours ago. We're at a physician's home. I talked to the doctor and he says you will be fine." Marius smiled softly.

"What happened?" I asked.

"You just got overexcited. You must have ridden too hard. Your heart was beating much too fast for your body to handle. It's actually not too uncommon. The less accustomed you are to working your body, the greater the chance that you'll overdo it. The only question is: why were you riding a horse in the middle of the woods?"

135

Sven and I exchanged glances. No longer did Sven seem bored. His eyes were wide open. Inherently we both knew that we should keep the tower a secret.

"I think that Rapunzel would appreciate some cold water, wouldn't you?" Sven stammered, trying to get Marius out of the room so that we could talk.

"Yes, that would be nice," I said, catching on.

Marius was smarter than Sven took him for. "I am sure you would not mind getting her some then."

Sven grimaced behind Marius' back and left the room. As soon as the door shut, Marius leaned in a little. "I have got to ask. Is he your lover?"

"My what?" I asked, shocked by his forwardness.

"I will take that as a resolute no. Does that mean that a young, single man such as I might perhaps have a chance?"

"I don't know." I looked away, my face hot. How could he be so bold as to ask such a thing?

"Would it help if I reminded you that I am mightily good-looking?" Marius asked, laughing. "You certainly are full of mysteries, Miss Rapunzel. Your hair, for starters: beautiful and yellow and long. I see how it disappears into that bag. Why do you hide it?"

Instinctively I felt the long golden locks. What was I going to say? I scrambled to think of a lie. The truth was ridiculous. How could I explain having seventy feet of hair?

"You do not really have to answer that. You wouldn't have done so honestly, would you?" Marius leaned back. "If Sven is not you lover, what is he?"

"Her friend." Sven walked back in with a glass full of water. "Well, almost friends, I suppose. As soon as I teach her to sword fight, we'll be friends. Isn't that right, Rapunzel?" Sven was making fun of Marius and all three of us knew it.

Marius stood and glared at Sven. The two contrasted sharply. Marius was taller than me, but still shorter than Sven. He seemed to be made to disappear into the streets. Sven stood out in any crowd. They were like night and day: both good by themselves, but not meant to mix on any occasion. The tension between the two was too troublesome for me.

"I think that I want to rest now, before we have to go," I said carefully.

"Of course." Sven set the water down and headed towards the door, grabbing Marius' arm to steer him the same way.

"One moment more," Marius said, carefully removing himself from Sven's grip. "I have one more question to ask." He paused. "Alone, if you don't mind."

Sven left willingly, if somewhat reluctantly.

Marius waited until he was gone. "Another thing, another question, if you do not mind." I shook my head. "Are you of noble blood?" Another shake. "Oh. I just assumed. Your hands are not hardened by work; your skin is light as if it never sees the sun." He stopped. "You are very mysterious, Miss Rapunzel." He walked out, leaving me alone.

I had not thought that I would actually be able to sleep, but as soon as the two men were gone, I could no longer keep my eyes open.

I awoke after not too long, wishing for company. There was a bell on the table next to me. When I rang, a young pretty woman appeared in the doorway. She was dressed in white robes that brushed the floor with a light whisper.

"Yes, Miss? Did you need something? Perhaps another pillow?" she asked, sweeping over to the bed.

"Oh, actually, I just wanted someone to talk to. Is that all right, or do you have something you need to be doing?" I sat up hopefully.

"Well," the girl started, seemingly undecided for a moment. She smiled, scurried to the door and peeked out before quickly shutting it, and sat down on the end of my bed. "If we're quiet enough, I don't think that anyone will miss me." She pulled her feet up and wrapped her arms around her legs in a tight lock. "I'm Chrissi. I'm training to be a physician here. It's my second year. I've been running about all day and I'm absolutely exhausted."

"Why are the walls black? Surely you know, having spent so much time here," I said. I had never heard of a room with black walls.

"It's to keep the bad spirits away. Brall, our physician, is very superstitious and he has this crazy theory that if the walls are black, any negative energy will be attracted away from the patients," she said sheepishly. "It may seem like a strange practice, but it has worked so far."

I was intrigued. I hadn't ever heard of someone doing that. My life in the tower seemed so monotonous compared to this town.

I fell asleep listening to stories about everyday life with the physician. Chrissi was all too happy to keep talking, regardless of whether or not I was listening. I got the impression that she didn't often have someone to speak to. I slept another few hours before Sven woke me and told me we had to leave if we were to get to the tower by sunset. He then left to go make sure the horses were ready.

Marius surprised me by stopping me before I had gotten out the door.

"I was glad that I could see you again today. Will you always visit me this often?" he asked.

I had to clear my head. Marius' words had a way of floating around in my thoughts and confusing me. "Perhaps, though I hope not in the same conditions next time." I reached for the door, thinking that Marius was finished.

"I will look for you." Marius leaned forward and quickly kissed my lips.

And suddenly everything was muddled. I was fairly certain that I saw Marius turn only to brush against the figure of Chrissi in the shadows, but that dropped into the back of my mind and was promptly forgotten. I went outside and mounted my horse. Resa whinnied softly.

"We'll take it slowly this time," Sven assured me as we set off. I barely heard him.

The rest of the trip blurred together. I climbed the tower, and it wasn't until I reached the top that I realized how sore my arms were.

"Don't come back tomorrow, I'm going to rest. Come back the next day, though," I called as I pulled the rope up.

"I should bring the supplies to teach you to sword fight, no?" he called.

"Yes! Yes, bring them!"

"All right then, I will." Sven turned Bruce around. Resa's reins were tied to Bruce's saddle. The three melted back into the trees, taking the last bits of sun with them.

It was about an hour later when Jacqueline came. She climbed my hair and we sat at the table to eat dinner together. She had rich yellow corn with her, still wrapped in its silky green clothing. We had often had it at the cottage, but since I had moved to the tower, we rarely did.

"I saw the most interesting thing the other day," Jacqueline commented lightly.

"Oh?" I asked.

"There was this cloud I saw. It looked just like an orange and I thought of you. I know that oranges are your favorite food."

"Oranges are circle. Most clouds look like that." I peered at her carefully with my eyebrows raised.

"Yes, but this one was orange and it made me think of you," she said. "It was the most interesting thing that I saw all day and I thought you'd like to hear."

I thought. I often wished that Jacqueline would come back with exciting stories from outside the tower, and when she never did, I had just assumed that nothing interesting ever happened. But today had proved me wrong. If I had been able to tell Jacqueline about my own adventure, I would have had many stories to share.

"Jacqueline, why don't you just climb a rope to get up here?" I asked.

Jacqueline blinked. She couldn't seem to think of anything to say. "No reason, dear. We don't even have any rope."

I winced inwardly. That's right. Sven had brought all of the rope. Jacqueline didn't know about it. I scrambled for words. "You could get some, is all I meant."

"I see. But aren't things fine the way they are? Nothing needs to change."

"I suppose so. Have you ever thought of letting me leave the tower? Just for a single day, not even long at all."

"Rapunzel, do not say such things! If I expose you to the evils of the world, you could be lost to me forever. There are all kinds of things out there. Wild animals, men, people who mean you harm. What would I do if some man came and swept you away?" Jacqueline stood, agitated.

My mind meandered to Sven and Marius. The spot on my lips where Marius had kissed me burned.

"I'm sorry. I will not bring it up again," I promised.

When Jacqueline left, I sat down right where I stood. Unfortunately, that happened to be right off to the side of my chair. I had to stop acting before I thought. I glared at the chair as if it was its fault that I hadn't sat in it.

I decided for sure that Jacqueline had cast a spell on the tower. The only way in was with my hair, unless a person could magic themselves out like Jacqueline. I didn't have a problem because my hair was a part of me. There was only one question remaining: how did Sven get in that night?

CHAPTER TEN

I was extremely grateful that I had taken a day to just rest at home. My arms felt like wet noodles left out in the heat. If only I had not been in the tower so long. If only I had enough muscle to climb without getting tired. If only I had room to run around so I would not get exhausted so easily.

"Stop it," I told myself. This would not do at all. I was drowning in a sea of "if only."

The day Sven came, I woke up early, but stayed in bed. It was too cold to leave the warmth of the covers just yet. When I heard his voice, I grudgingly crawled out and got dressed.

As I slid down the rope to the ground, I mentally noted that I wanted gloves. I was getting a burn from where the rope bit my fingers. They shone a brilliant red, pretty but painful.

Sven had only brought Bruce this time. We would not need Resa. He had two swords, both covered in a wooden casing, and two bows, each with their own quiver full of arrows.

"You ready?" Sven asked.

"I think so. What are we doing first?" I shifted my weight back and forth, my fingers itching to rush over and try everything out.

"Your pick." He swept his arm over to the pile of weapons.

"I say... sword." How exciting would it be if I were to learn to wield a sword?

Sven picked up the swords and held one of the carefully out to me. I reached eagerly for it, but he pulled it back before I could get a hold on the wood. "You do understand that this is a real sword underneath the cover, don't you?" he asked.

"Yes, I do. Now give it here." I reached for it again, but Sven kept it resolutely out of my grasp.

"No, I don't think you quite understand. If you hit me with this, or the other way around, it can bruise and it will. You could even break a bone, got it?" He looked extremely concerned that I was going to hurt him.

I sighed and snatched the sword. It was heavier that I had expected, but I could hold it in both hands without too much trouble. I pointed it out and swatted away an imaginary foe.

"Take that!" I swung again. "And that!" I hit a tree and fell over.

Sven helped me up, dusted me off and pulled on the sword. It stayed stuck in between two close branches. He grumbled a moment, then braced himself against the tree and pulled. With a loud crack, the sword dislodged.

"Try again," he said, handing it back to me. "This time move away from the trees, and only use one hand."

It was more easily said than done. The sword point shook in my grasp. Sven made me hold it out straight. When I could hold the blade relatively still, Sven got out his to teach me different techniques. I quickly found that I had absolutely no talent for sword fighting. Sven taught me the basics: to parry, to block and to thrust, but when he asked me to repeat the exercise, I tripped over my own feet.

"One more time, Rapunzel. You will get it this time," Sven said.

"That is what you said last time," I said breathless. Nevertheless, I tried again. Parry. Block. Block. Block.

Thrust. Sven rapped my knuckles with his sword. Though it was covered in wood, the long weapon still hurt.

"Maybe it's your hair," Sven said after I flumped down on the ground. "It's probably harder to be light on your feet when you have fifty pounds of hair on your back."

"I can't actually feel its weight." I did not sit up, preferring to stare at the clouds. "I was not made to sword fight, I guess."

"Lots of people were not made to use a sword. A bow on the other hand, well, everyone can learn to shoot an arrow. Even if you never become amazing at it, merely rudimentary skills would be useful. You don't have to able to shoot an apple off of someone's head; you just have to be able to hit a stump."

He gently took the sword from my hand. It was replaced with a slick dark brown bow and a quiver of arrows. The brown and white feathers tickled my chin. The weapon was obviously made for someone larger and stronger than me. It felt awkward in my hands as I positioned it the way Sven was showing me. I pulled the string back, feeling it squish my nose flat as I had been told, and aimed straight ahead. Sven said that I shouldn't worry about hitting a target just yet, so I was not concerned about exactly where I my arrow was going to end up. As I let go, my eyes squeezed shut.

Sven yelled. I opened my eyes and looked at him. He was pinned against a tree, the arrow thrust through his shoulder. I yelled too. The bow dropped from my fingers as I ran over. Sven was breathing heavily, but smiling. He looked at me apologetically. I stared. How could he be happy? What was good about this situation?

"I'm– I'm fine," he wheezed, his breathing turning into a fit of laughter. "It didn't get me. I'm fine."

It took me a few moments to understand. Sven reached over and yanked the arrow out. I flinched. He held it up to me. There was no blood; the arrow had pierced his shirt. It had missed his skin by the smallest space.

"You're fine?" I breathed.

"Absolutely. I think I've learned to stay out of your way. I wasn't expecting you to aim at me, and so I wasn't paying attention to where you were aiming. I'll find a target this time, and you," he paused. "Just try to keep your eyes open." He pointed at me as he said it, shaking just a bit.

We found something for me to aim at. The target was a marked tree about ten paces away. It was promptly filled with two arrows. Neither of them were anywhere near the center. Indeed, none of them even hit their mark straight on, sitting instead all crooked.

For the third time, I took an arrow from my quiver and placed it in the correct spot. I slowly pulled the string back and took aim.

"Hold it steady. Don't rush it," Sven said.

I breathed in slowly and released the arrow.

It flew seemingly straight until it hit the bark directly above the target. I winced. That's what happened every time. I thought everything was going fine until I let go.

"So close, again." Sven pulled the arrow out of the tree.

"I'm definitely getting worse," I said. "This isn't helping at all. Everything is too big. I need something smaller." My arms hurt from drawing back the string even a few times.

"I can't think of anything like that." Sven gathered up all of the wayward arrows and stuck them in the quiver. "Wait, maybe I have something that will work." He bent down and pulled a small dagger out of his pocket. "It's not the most common thing in the world, but I find that it is just as effective as a sword or a bow."

The blade was about five inches long, the bejeweled hilt an additional three. It looked like a small version of Sven's sword. The gold, the emeralds, this was made for Sven.

"Here, throw this." He held it out to me.

I didn't take it. "You keep a knife in your boot?" I didn't think that anyone really did that. Maybe it was a way that boys made themselves feel tougher than they were.

Sven placed the knife in my hand and closed my fingers around it softly. "Throw it." He pointed me in the direction of the target. There was no point in arguing. He would just bother me until I did what he said. I adjusted my fingers until they felt comfortable: thumb and first finger near the blade, last three fingers toward the back.

"Move your first finger a little," Sven advised. "It's bound to go wrong if you hold it like that."

I acted as if I did not hear him and threw the knife as hard as I could, flicking it as I did to make it spin. I squeezed my eyes shut instinctively; I was sure it was going to be off course.

Thunk. At least it hit the tree. I could not gather up the courage to look.

Sven whistled, low and long. When he did not comment, I peeked up and blinked a few times, surprised at what I saw.

The knife's blade had embedded itself halfway up to the hilt in the wood, right on target.

I turned to Sven. He stared disbelievingly at me.

"You are such a liar. I thought that you had never done this before. You've been keeping secrets from me," he said.

"I have not," I said.

"But– but– you just– a perfect shot– first time?" Sven had the bright spark of an idea in his eye as he stuttered. "This is brilliant. There is so much that you can do with this. Different distances, sizes, anything!"

I patiently listened as Sven grew more and more excited about my newfound ability. After a while, I stopped listening and sat down. He was going to keep talking whether or not I paid attention. I assumed that he would move on soon, but he didn't. I began tracing shapes in the dirt.

"Let's talk about this later, shall we?" I interjected.

Sven stopped midsentence. "Oh. Why?"

"I'm hungry, and it is time to eat." I stood and headed toward the tower. Sven did not follow. "Are you coming?" I asked, the desire to eat overcoming all else.

"Yes." He came after me.

I climbed up the rope. This time was easier than before. I was getting better at climbing without needing to depend so heavily on the rope. I used mainly the stones and cracks in between them. As I started to pull it to me, Sven grabbed it.

"Aren't you forgetting something?" he asked, trying to pull the end of the rope back down to him. His grip was stronger and I let go.

I thought a bit. "No," I said. "Not anything I can think of."

"What about me? I get to come up there, right? You're going to feed me too."

"Yes, I suppose, but you can't climb up the rope."

"What? Then how exactly am I supposed to get up there? Fly? I know that I'm skilled in almost every other aspect of life, but I haven't managed to fly yet. It's disappointing, I know."

My hair tumbled down to answer him. "I will explain when you get up," I said.

"Last time I tried climbing up your hair, you punched me," Sven mumbled as he started up. "Let's not repeat that little episode. I must say, this way is certainly easier."

"That's the spirit." I pulled back from the window.

When Sven reached the top and climbed inside, he wandered around the room. I pulled my hair inside, watching him carefully. Making sure to keep my hair away from his feet, I gathered it up so it would be out of his way.

"It is a lot bigger than it looks from the outside, isn't it?" he commented. "I thought that it would be very cramped inside. That's what you get, living with a witch."

"Well, I suppose so. It has been a very long time since I have lived anywhere else." I shrugged. "The cottage near the village was a long time ago, as I'm sure you remember."

"So tell me, why is it that I can't climb up the rope like you do?" He sat on the floor, easily making himself comfortable.

I sat in front of him, my legs crossed underneath me. "Magic." I waited his reaction.

Sven raised his eyebrows. "You really resent giving me a straight answer don't you?"

That hadn't been the response I was seeking. Even at the village, I had remembered most people being impressed by magic in any form. "I did just give you a straight answer. Jacqueline cast a spell on the tower. The only way you can get in is with the magical aid my hair gives," I said.

"I guess that explains why she makes you grow your hair so long." Sven paused. "No, that's not right. That can't be right. I got in alone. I climbed up the rope and got in all by myself. Don't tell me you've already forgotten that night. You hit me on the head with a book, but I got through the window just fine."

"That is what's confusing me. Did you feel anything when you came in?"

Sven thought, frowning. "I'm not sure. Wait, yes, as a matter of fact, I did. There was this sharp pain as I passed through the window. It felt like I was trying to cross through a wall of thistles. I shoved against it and I was through. It was as simple as that. There was nothing else to suggest that I had passed through a spell."

"Odd, maybe it was just a fluke. I wouldn't try it again if I were you." I sat next to him. Most of my hair coiled over my lap. "What if the magic actually hurt you next time?"

"What is this? Are you actually showing some kindness towards me?" Sven asked.

"No." I turned to him. "I just don't know what I would do with your body if you died up here. You are far too heavy for me to lift."

Sven picked up a length of my hair. He ran his fingers through it. I could almost feel his touch. It sent shivers down my spine.

"So, are you going to tell me about your father? Don't you miss him?"

I had thought that Sven had forgotten about asking that question.

"I don't know what to say. There are no memories in my mind of him," I said slowly, carefully.

"What happened to him?"

"I am not sure. I suppose he left when I was born, maybe even much before that. That or he died. Either way, it's not a good thought. It's much easier just to forget about him and move on." I felt a little bad for saying that, but I didn't know how to take it back. I didn't know if I wanted to take it back.

Sven was silent.

"Stop touching my hair." I slapped his hands and yanked it at it, but Sven just pulled me towards him. We sat side by side.

"So if you cut your hair, no one would ever be able to get up?" Sven asked thoughtfully. He tactfully dropped the subject of my father.

"Unless that person is you." I bumped his shoulder with my own.

"Yes, unless they are me," Sven agreed.

"I wonder why you were able to get through the magic," I said. I thought of something else. "Why did you work so hard to get up?"

"What do you mean by that?" Sven avoided my gaze.

"Most people would have just given up when I did not let them in at first, wouldn't they? Why go through all that trouble?"

Sven didn't speak. He looked bashful. "No reason," he eventually said

"There is a reason. I can see it in your face."

"No, there is not."

"Yes—"

"I don't want to talk about it, all right?" Sven stood. "Maybe it's time for me to go."

I wound my hair around the hook and let Sven climb down. Before he reached the bottom, I thought of something.

"You have to come back sometime, you know. We're friends now. Friends do that for each other," I reminded him.

He smiled and shook his head. I could tell that he was trying not to laugh at me. "I will not forget."

I thought about Sven and Marius. I knew that it was wrong to compare them, they were so different, but I could not help it. Anyway, I was going to have to pick one of them sooner or later, wasn't I?

CHAPTER ELEVEN

"Don't you ever get bored in here?" Sven asked.

I shrugged. "I guess, but really, I have a lot to do." I gestured to my books. Sven wandered over to the shelves. "I've read all of them," I said proudly, locating my favorites as I stood behind him.

Sven ran his fingers over the spines, and picked one out, lifting it gently. I recognized it as my songbook. As he moved to open it, I tried to distract him and take it back.

"You don't want that. It's boring."

Sven held it out of my reach and started to read. "Did you write these?" he asked.

I stopped trying to grab it, he was too much taller than I was. Sven walked over to a chair and sat down, reading my songs. I sat on a chair next to him and sulked. I didn't want him reading them; they weren't very good. When he finished, he set it carefully back onto my shelf. I noticed that he had put it in the exact same place as before. That was a good thing because all the books were in a certain order.

"What's this?" he asked, peering at something else.

I walked over and stifled a laugh. It was the Rodian dictionary, the same one that I had hit him with. He made the connection a moment after he spoke. With a low grunt, he lifted the book off of the shelf and hauled it over to the table.

"No wonder you knocked me out. How did you manage to lift it? Your arms are so skinny," he muttered.

I just sat and stared. What a strange, strange man. Half the time, I couldn't decide if he was speaking to me or not.

"Can you speak it?" he asked suddenly.

I didn't follow for a moment, but then I saw his gaze travel to the dictionary. "Oh, do I speak Rodian? I do, a little, I guess." I wasn't very good at picking up on the complicated words, but I could say a few things. "Do you?"

"Yes." Sven laughed. "I suppose that I could probably remember how to say a few things." Something about the way he said it made me think that I was missing some kind of joke.

Sven came almost every day now. I enjoyed his company, but sometimes I wasn't quite sure what he was talking about. He had a funny way of speaking, or he had a funny way of phrasing things, rather. It was as if he was not always sure he was using the right words. And sometimes he seemed to be talking to himself.

BOOM, thunder sounded. I thought that I was ready for spring to be over. I was sick of these storms, but I still couldn't resist the rain. As always, I raced to the window and leaned out, smelling the clean, electric smell of the water. I wished that I could be in it. Then I realized that I could.

"Sven, come outside with me!" I called. I turned, Sven had accidently knocked the book to the ground, though I didn't know why.

Sven picked the dictionary and raised his eyebrow. "Why?"

"I want to go dance in the rain!" I said excitedly. I wanted to feel mud in between my toes. I wanted my hair to get soaked; I wanted to taste the rain.

Sven considered. I could see that he was going to say no, and so I quickly rushed over and grabbed his arm. "Come on! It'll be fun, you'll see." Sven rolled his eyes and stood.

"I'll come with you," he said grudgingly. I thought that he might be shaking but I wasn't sure.

The rain felt deliciously cool. Once we were down from the tower, I carefully dug my toes into the wet, soft ground. Mud oozed up, covering my light skin in a brown coating. I spread my arms out and tipped my head back, catching raindrops in my mouth.

Sven, on the other hand, huddled under a tree, arms crossed, trying to keep as much out of the rain as possible. At first I thought that he shied from the water because the last time he had been in it, he had fallen off his horse and gotten lost. After a while, I realized that it was more than that. Sven was afraid of the rain.

"You're going to catch a cold," he said.

"I'll be fine. Why don't you come and join me?" I asked. Something was wrong. Sven was not scared of anything. How could something so small worry him?

"No, I don't think I will." Sven leaned even more against the tree. "You know, I'll just leave. I have things to do." He started to walk into the trees.

Lightning streaked across the sky, lighting up everything around us spectacularly. I only had eyes for Sven. however. When the accompanying thunder sounded, he cringed so violently that he fell to his knees.

"Are you all right?" I called, running over. I sat next to him, ignoring the cold forest floor beneath me. "Sven, what's wrong?"

He was leaning over as if someone had punched his stomach. His eyes were squeezed shut, his fingernails dug into his forehead. He muttered darkly. I tried to understand what he said, but soon I realized the he spoke another language. I thought that it might be Rodian. My suspicions were confirmed when I heard the Rodian word for witch.

"Sven, what's wrong?" I asked. He didn't answer. "Sven." I grabbed his hands and pulled them from his skin. He wouldn't look at me. "Sven, come back." I shook his shoulders. Suddenly he looked up. It took a few moments for him to really see me.

"Oh. Oh, I'm sorry, that was foolish. I'm fine," he said halfheartedly.

"Don't lie. What happened? You can speak Rodian. You speak it perfectly," I flinched at the incoherency of my speech.

Sven looked up for a moment, and then met my eyes again. "Yes, I do. I was born there," he said. I let him talk uninterrupted, afraid that if he stopped, he would never start again. "My mother and I lived alone; my father had left years earlier. My mother was a witch. We lived far away from other people just outside of Goadliton. They feared her as they feared her magic. One day, they came. Usually we ran when this happened, and we would be left alone for a while, but we didn't hear them until it was too late."

"I didn't ever think that they would hurt her. I never thought..." He had to stop for a minute. "But I was stupid. They threw us out into the downpour. One man said to my mother that I had betrayed her, that I had led them to her. I don't know why she believed them. She was a witch in a world that feared magic, and I suppose the fear made her irrational. She cursed me. The words she said made me afraid. I ran through the rain, as far away as I could go. Perhaps I could have helped her, but I was too scared."

I wanted to say something that would make him better, but nothing came to mind. I knew that there wasn't anything that I could do.

Sven didn't see me struggle for words. He stared off into empty air for a minute and laughed bitterly. "I ran until my feet bled. I knew few people, and none of them would take me in. I'm not sure when I crossed the border. One day I came to a town and I could hear people speaking, but their words made no sense. I sat back and listened, learning the language. I stayed close to the border where the dialects made the most sense to me. After a few years, I ended up in Salae. It didn't take long for them to realize that there was something wrong with me." He laughed again, making me shiver. "I was cursed, diseased, and by my own mother even. In Salae, when I found out there was another witch, I was so scared. If she was anything like my mother, I didn't want to be anywhere nearby her. After that night, I was left with a terror of witches and an irrational fear of the rain. It's stupid, I know."

I didn't say anything. What could I possibly say? What he had told me explained his dislike of Jacqueline, but I knew that there was so much he wasn't telling me. I could see it in his eyes. He had made it sound much less painful than it had been.

"Someday you will tell me the full story," I said, shivering. The rain had been so refreshing at first, but now it was almost painful. My clothes stuck to my skin, my hair plastered heavily to my face.

"Someday," he murmured. "But not for a long time." He looked over at me and saw my teeth chattering. "You're going to freeze," he said.

"I'll be perfectly all right," I argued

Sven was back to normal. He touched my forehead and drew back. "You're getting a fever." He picked me up against my will and got me into the tower.

CHAPTER TWELVE

Sven must have been right, because for the next two days I was horribly sick. My throat felt coated in a thick slime and my head was filled with a throbbing that kept me up in the night. My body was attacking me from all sides.

For those two days, I refused Sven entry into the tower. I did, however, remember to send him food so that he wouldn't starve. Jacqueline would come each evening and feed me soup. She kept asking how I managed to get sick. I didn't have an answer, at least, not one that I wanted to tell her. On the morning of the third day, Sven refused to leave.

"You can't stay up there forever," he said.

Just watch me. I rolled over in bed, miserable. "Yes I can," I croaked.

"I am trying to save you from being even more of a recluse than you already are, and I would appreciate it if you would help me."

With a groan, I rolled out of bed and made my way to the window, stumbling over everything in my path.

Sven came up, took one look at me and sighed. "I had hoped that I would be able to get you to sing for me, but I now I realize that's probably not going to happen. I guess I will have to display one of my own talents."

I crawled back into bed. "Oh, and what talents are those?" I grumbled, burrowing under the covers, leaving my head barely visible, propped up on the pillows behind me.

"I am sure that you would rather guess than have me simply hand you the answers." Sven wandered the room.

"I am not going to guess."

"Then I am not going to tell. Your loss, really, I am very talented."

I tried not to give in, but eventually my curiosity got the better of me. "You juggle," I guessed.

"Do I?" Sven picked up three apples from the kitchen table. "Here I go." He started to throw them in the air. At first, I thought that he was doing rather well, but after three throws, he threw one too high and it landed on his head.

"Well, you are certainly not a juggler." I thought. What else could he be? "You are a gymnast. If you had not met the king, you would have joined up with a traveling freak show to be a contortionist. Is that it?"

Sven was not flexible. He could not even manage to touch his toes. Nor could he sing, act, or sew. He did not carve wood or stone, and there was no doubt that he was not a dancer—not without a partner, anyway.

I noticed that Sven kept glancing at my canvas and oil paints. They lay somewhat abandoned on the floor. His fingers twitched. He wanted to go and examine the paint, but he forced himself not to even move towards them.

An idea came to me. "An artist! You are a painter!"

"Bravo!" Sven bowed. "Does this mean that you are inviting me to test those beautiful paintbrushes of yours?"

He did not even wait for an answer. Rather, he walked very quickly over there. As he picked up a fresh canvas, he uncovered the bird painting I had started. His face brightened. "Ah, it is your lobster. If I were you, I would have thrown this away," he said. "No, I would've buried it. This really is dreadful."

"It's not a lobster. It is supposed to be a bird," I explained.

"Really?" He looked closer at it. "Yes, I think that you should stick with your singing for now. It seems to be working out a lot better for you."

He set the canvas on my easel and settled onto the stool in front of it. As I watched, he stared critically at the empty space, turning his head from side to side.

"What are you going to paint?" I asked. Not willing to leave the comfort of my bed, I lied down on my stomach at the end of it, my feet on my pillow.

"Not quite sure," he mumbled, still intent on the canvas. "Whatever the canvas wants to become."

I didn't quite understand, but I was quiet as he thought.

Then, suddenly, he started to move the brush across the page. Blue stripes appeared behind his strokes. His hand moved quickly. He was perfectly sure of himself and there was no hesitation in his movements.

Blue, green, yellow, colors in between that I could not even name magically took form on the canvas.

The first things that I recognized were trees, tall trees. It was a forest set some time in between winter and spring, when the leaves were just being born. Sven turned and saw me staring. He shifted so he blocked his work.

"It has to be a surprise or it is no fun," he said.

"Ugh. I don't want to have fun; I just want to see what you are drawing!"

"Hmm. Well, you do not exactly have a choice, now do you? In any case, I wasn't talking about fun for you. I meant that it would be no fun for me."

I was tempted to throw a pillow at him. I did not, for I feared to smudge the paint, but it was tempting. Perhaps after he was done, I would throw one at him.

After the first couple of minutes, Sven began mumbling to himself. "That is not quite right, higher, no, that's wrong.... A bit darker, I think." He went on and on.

I had been waiting long enough that my eyes had begun to droop and I might have even fallen asleep when Sven said calmly, but with excitement in his voice, "Come and see it."

I swung off my bed, stood and approached the drying painting to get a better look. I peered closely to see what it was.

It was me. I was in the forest I had seen him painting before. I was dwarfed by the trees as they reached their leafy arms towards the heavens. It could have either been the morning or the start of evening. I decided that it was early morning because of the many birds that appeared to be waking in the trees. It was almost as if I could hear them singing.

I was in a blue dress, with long trailing sleeves. He had gotten my hair just right. For the first foot or so, it hung untamed. The rest of my braid curled around my feet and trailed off of the edge of the painting. The yellow hair sparkled brightly as if it were gold. The eyes were what caught my gaze. They were so intense, staring resolutely to the right. Their green hue startled even me. There was a dagger gripped firmly in my left hand. It was gold with green gems. It was Sven's knife without a doubt.

"It's– it's–" It was magnificent beyond words. How on earth could he have done all of that in such a short span of time?

"I thought that you would like a portrait of yourself to keep, seeing as you don't have any. It is not too strange for me to have done, is it?"

"No, not at all. I'm just, amazed, that's all. It is very beautiful."

Sven smiled. "I am glad that you like it."

There was a sound from deep within the forest. I ran to the window. Jacqueline was coming from not too far away.

"Jacqueline!" I did the first thing I thought of. I grabbed an apple from the bowl by my bed and threw it at Bruce. It hit him on the head. I said a silent apology as he reared in fright.

"What are you doing? Have you gone mad? That's my horse! How am I going to leave now?" Sven asked when Bruce galloped away.

I pulled the rope up. "There's no time for you to leave. She'll see you. You have to hide." I managed to remain remarkably calm on the outside, despite the panic rising in my throat.

Sven looked around. "Where am I going to hide?"

"Under the bed. Take the painting with you." I started cleaning up all of the paint supplies.

Sven squeezed under my bed on his stomach, pushing the beautiful painting with him. I was glad that I had such a large bed.

"Rapunzel! Let down your hair to me," called Jacqueline's voice.

I checked to see that Sven was hidden. There was no sign of him. I let down my hair. When Jacqueline reached the top, she looked suspiciously around.

"Jacqueline." I moved to embrace her.

She pulled away, staring over my shoulder into the room. "Something is not right," she said. She seemed to be trying to hear something. I knew that she was going to find Sven if I didn't stop her somehow.

"No, nothing is wrong. Everything is fine," I lied.

"There is something off, I know it," she said insistently.

To my horror, Jacqueline began to search my room. She peeked into my closet, pushing aside clothes. The only thing that emerged was Jean Claude, barking happily. I had no idea how he had gotten in there. As Jacqueline slowly made her way to my bed, my mind raced as I thought how to distract her.

"What are you looking for?" I asked, casually trying to squeeze between her and Sven.

"I am not sure, but I will know it when I find it."

"I did see something, out on a hill not too far away. A horse, with a rider, I think." The words burst from my mouth before I had time to think about them.

"You saw what?" Jacqueline spun on me.

"A person on a horse," I said softly, suddenly doubting the wisdom of my words.

"Where?" She swept to the window.

"Umm… to the east. He came with the sun this morning." I was getting better at lying, but I still had not had much practice and I was sure that Jacqueline would find me out.

She must have been too agitated to listen properly. "I have to find this person. Let me down, Rapunzel. I will not be back for a few days. Do not worry about me," she said.

"Jacqueline, what if it was a man? Do you think I could meet him?" I asked. It was worth a shot. "Maybe it would be good for me to have a companion. It's just been you and me for so long."

"If it is a man, coming this close to you, I swear on my life, I will kill him. So help me, I will."

When she was gone, I went over to where Sven was lying on the floor, staring wide-eyed ahead. In his gaze, I could almost see the memories of his mother cursing him.

"She's gone," I confirmed.

He shimmied out, pulling the portrait with him again. His face was ghostly white.

"I think that it would be a bad thing if she found out that you were here," I said and took the portrait from him. "You have dust in your hair," I added, absentmindedly.

"You think?" Sven rubbed his hands through his hair, making gray dust particles go everywhere. I could see goose bumps covering his arms up and down.

"She really is a good person. Just too overprotective, you see."

"Tell me, Rapunzel, how do you like it, living with a witch? Knowing that she could probably fry your insides with only a glance?" He took a breath. "Knowing that she would without a second thought. I know," said Sven bitterly. I knew that he had a grudge against witches, but I hated his comment. I loved Jacqueline.

"You do not know everything, Sven. She is not a bad person. What about you?"

"What about me?"

"What is it like, living in an enormous, beautiful castle with butlers and maids waiting on you? What is it like to be able to go anywhere you would like and have people hang on your every word? It must be terrible, to have the life everyone dreams about." I turned my head so that I would not have to look at him.

There was no sound but the birds in the trees for a long time. I could not quite understand why I was so argumentative with Sven. Something about the two of us just did not work.

I suddenly knew that he was right behind me. I could feel him hesitating next to me. I did not move, and neither did he.

"Tell me about it," I said.

Sven knew what I was talking about. He sighed. "In the morning, light shoots through my window and brightens up my room like a candle. I get up every day and sneak out of my room through a hidden panel in the wall in order to avoid the servants. I head straight for the kitchens to meet up with William, my very best friend, the only person I can really talk to.

"And the gardens, oh, you would love them. There's a giant maze made of hedges, and in the middle of the maze, there are flowers, orchards, vegetable gardens. The birds are absolutely everywhere. They build giant nests in the trees, some as big as wagon wheels."

I spun to face him. "Is William the friend you are looking for? The one you were talking about, the kitchen boy?"

"Yes. A few weeks ago he disappeared. I have been looking for him ever since."

"I've been distracting you." I felt horrible. I had been selfishly hoarding his attention while his friend needed help.

"No, I have been looking, maybe a little less vigorously, but I have been studying your maps and I think that I have an idea of where he might be. I plan on leaving to find him soon."

"I'm going to come with you," I said.

"No, you are not."

"I am. How are you planning on stopping me?"

"I'll... use your own hair to tie you up until I come back," Sven threatened, picking up a section of hair to demonstrate.

"I doubt that would work." I sat down, folded my arms and crossed my legs. "In fact, I would like to see you try."

"Really? Fine. Let's see here. Stay there, and do not move," Sven said. "Where's the end of this mess?" He meant my hair.

"I have no idea. You will just have to figure it out yourself." I smirked. "Good luck."

Sven picked up a section of braid and started to follow it around the room. He dramatically sighed every time he had to move something out of his way. When he found the end, he held it above his head in triumph. "Success!" he shouted. As he lugged my hair over, he groaned comically. "This stuff is hard to move. How do you even walk?"

I shrugged vaguely. "Superior skill, I suppose."

Sven did his best to successfully secure me to the chair, I am sure that he did. I'm also sure that it would've been fine if he were using rope rather than hair. When it came down to it, my hair was nothing like rope. Hair had a different grip to it. You had to tie it in a way which would prevent it from slipping; a way that a man would most likely not have any practice in.

"Done. Let's see you get out of that," Sven said when he was satisfied.

I wiggled a bit. Jean Claude, on the floor next to me, imitated my movements, wiggling slightly.

"Not so clever now, are you?" Sven asked.

I wiggled a bit more. His main knot started to slip. Once the knot had shifted, the entire thing came undone.

I stood, stepped out of the tangled mess of hair and spread my arms dramatically.

"Ta-da!" I said.

"What? How did you manage to do that?" Sven asked.

"You tied your knots entirely wrong."

"And how would you do it?" Sven looked a bit downcast, but still sure that I would not be able to accomplish what he could not.

I grabbed his shoulders and forced him into the chair.

"Sit still and watch the master at work. Master, that's not right. Master-ess?" I waved the matter away.

It took me precisely five minutes to adequately tie Sven into a suitable bind.

"All right. It's your turn. I don't think that there is any way you will be able to work your way out." I sat on the bed. This was going to take quite a while.

"This will be easy. Come one, Rapunzel, you could at least try to give me a–" He cut off when he could not immediately free himself.

"Something wrong? Not quite as easy as you thought that it was going to be, is it?" I smiled.

Sven glanced my way. "Oh, it'll be easy. I am just trying to make you feel good about yourself and your rather juvenile knot tying."

"Oh, well thank you for your consideration, but just get on with it, won't you?" I said.

Sven moved a bit. "Now, the trick is to go slow, you see? To just work your way out inch by inch." He tried to demonstrate for me. The knots did not budge.

"I could save you a lot of time by telling you now that you are not going to be able to get out," I said.

Of course, Sven didn't listen to me. "And I will suggest that you save your breath. Now hush up and let me concentrate."

"Why would you need to concentrate? I thought that you said this would be easy."

"It is going to be easy, I just– I don't have to explain myself to you." He spotted the old grandfather clock on the side of my closet. "Time me. It will take but five minutes for me to get free. Then you will see." Sven nodded at me. "Go on, start counting."

Five minutes into Sven's attempt to escape, he had not made any progress.

Six minutes passed, nine minutes passed. When the clock hit ten minutes, I turned to smile at Sven.

"Just a couple more minutes," he muttered.

Fifteen minutes, twenty minutes. Half an hour after I had originally started keeping track of the time, and twenty minutes after his self-appointed deadline, Sven was still hopelessly trapped.

"All right Rapunzel. You win," he sighed. Poor Sven had defeat written all over his face.

"Really?" I asked, unable to keep the smug tone out of my voice.

"I can't believe that I couldn't untie a simple knot tied by a girl."

"Not just any girl. A girl who spends her days alone, with no experience in tying anything but what she does with her hair," I reminded him.

"No need to rub it in."

"So are you ready to listen to reason?" I asked.

"Only if you are ready to speak reason," he said.

"You are so charming." I walked forward. "You are going to let me come with you. We are going to look for William together."

"No."

"Yes. I am going with you."

"No, you're not."

"How do you expect to go anywhere then?" I asked.

Sven looked skeptical. "And what does that mean?"

"I mean that you're not moving from that chair until you agree to let me help you."

"You would have to let me free sooner or later." Sven said the words confidently enough, but his face betrayed his doubt.

"No, I really don't have to ever let you go. What would make you think that?" I asked.

"You can't just leave me here forever."

"Why ever not? I live here. My hair is long enough that I don't have to ever untie you. I can go anywhere in the tower without worrying about you."

"You are so agitating," groaned Sven.

"That doesn't matter. I am in control, and you have to do what I say."

"Fine. Let's go to Acada, pick up some supplies," Sven started.

See Marius.

"Buy a few more detailed maps," he continued.

Talk to Marius.

"We'll go a few days of searching, and then I will take you back." He wiggled, not even budging. "Will you let me out now?"

I tugged the tiniest bit on a strand of hair. The knot fell apart, and my hair lay at Sven's feet.

"That took two seconds. I don't think that I am ever going to be able to get my self-esteem back up again." Sven stood and brushed himself off, looking for stray hairs.

"It is going to be an adventure, Sven! I've always wanted to go on an adventure!" I bounced slightly.

"An adventure, yes, I'm sure." Sven's expression did not embody an attitude of excitement but I ignored that.

CHAPTER THIRTEEN

It took only a few minutes for Sven to lose his gloomy mood. He made me ride on Bruce right in front of him. The look on my face was clearly enough to get him to smile.

"Will can't be far. There is no way that we are going to have to search more than a twenty mile radius," he said.

"Twenty miles? That's small?" I asked.

"For as long as he had been missing, yes, that is a small distance," Sven explained.

"Sven, doesn't anyone miss you at the castle? You have been gone for a long time, what about the king?"

He laughed lightly. "Rapunzel, just how much do you know about Dao?"

"It's the capitol of Ordainia. It is near the south-west border of the kingdom. The main crop is peppermint, a favorite of the king's."

"You know more than you think," he said. "But not as much as you should."

"And what should I know?" I hated these conversations that we had while riding Bruce, but something in Sven's tone of voice warned me that he needed to say this now.

"Dao is the center of everything in this country. King Blasé is a good ruler, when it comes to external affairs, anyhow. In the city itself, the king's eye hardly falls there. It was the queen's job to take care of the city and the people, and when she died, the king never picked up her duties. He's got officers to watch things for him. The streets are relatively clean, but crime has recently started to rise, and yet the king's footsteps never grace the market's cobblestones. What must the people think? That their king doesn't care?

"The castle is cold and rather empty. I always imagined that where the king lived would be bright and busy, swarming with people bustling about like bees. But no, it's often dark. There are few candles and lanterns ever lit, you see." Sven took a deep breath. "The King does not often ask for my presence. I doubt that he even notices that I am gone, especially now. He has been ill recently, and may very well still be in bed."

"Oh, Sven. I am so sorry." The idea of not having anyone who loved you was foreign to me. I had always had Jacqueline; I had never been alone.

"Don't be. I am used to it, and I have Will." His voice caught in his throat.

"We will find him. He will be fine," I said.

"I have to. We told each other everything; girls we had met, the things they had said. We were–are–closer than brothers. In a sense we are brothers, brothers in blood anyway." He held out his right hand; there was a long scar across it.

The rest of the ride was in an uncomfortable silence.

"Where is Resa?" I asked. I really needed to ride my own horse if Sven was going to insist that we ride the stupid animals.

"Don't worry; we're going to get her from the stables. I know that you did not want to ride with me the entire time."

We entered through Acada's gates.

"I bet if you were with Marius, you would be fine with staying on the same horse," Sven commented lightly. My face colored. Luckily, Sven couldn't see the signs of my embarrassment. "You get off here, and just hang around for a few hours while I go scout out some supplies. I'll meet you in the stables." He nudged me. "Go on, go on."

I slid delicately off of Bruce. I made it to the ground without too much panic, but I still disliked it.

"Where do I find the stables?" I asked.

"Follow that small road south." Sven pointed. "Do you see it?"

I craned my neck and caught sight of what he was referring to.

"If you follow it about five hundred feet, the stables will be on your left. It's a large building and hard to miss."

"What if I get lost?" I shifted uncomfortably. "I don't want to just wait in the stables for the entire time you are gone."

"All right, fine. On the main road, the white cobblestones are intermixed with black ones. If you follow that road, either way you go, you will eventually stumble upon the stables," Sven reassured me.

"I just need to follow the black stones?" I thought that it seemed easy enough, but that didn't mean I couldn't get lost. I was really good at getting lost.

"Yes. That's it. It would be much faster to take the first route, but for you, I believe that the main road may be safer."

Sven started to ride away. He looked back. "Watch out for thieves. They prey on people like you." He was talking about Marius.

As Sven left, I checked to make sure that my bag was properly closed. There wasn't really anything for anybody to steal. The only thing concealed in there was my overly long hair, wrapped around itself again and again.

Of course, thieves would not know that. For all they know, you could have anything in there. I thought about what Marius had asked me. *What if someone else thinks that you are noble too?*

"Ah, my lovely lady, how would you like a new bracelet? A beautiful piece of jewelry for a beautiful woman."

I turned to see a man in a long black coat and a hat tipped over his face. He lifted the hat away and swept a low bow. It was Marius. He held out a silver metal bracelet. I took it, staring in wonder. It wrapped around in a circle five times, curving up and down about a quarter inch. Tiny runes were inscribed across the entire surface.

"I– I– I–" My attempt to form words stumbled out my mouth.

"Just put it on," Marius prompted. It fit perfectly. "It's the real thing. Pure silver," he said.

"Where did you get it?" A terrible thought came to my mind. "You did not steal it, did you?" I put my hand to the silver, ready to pull it off.

"No, of course not!" Marius pulled my hand away.

"Then how could you afford something like this?"

"Rapunzel, I got it honestly. My mother left it for me," he said. "She told me before she died that I should give it to a girl I thought was beautiful."

I raised my eyebrows. "For a thief, you are a bad liar."

"If I do not tell you, then you don't have to worry. And I'm not going to tell you anything because you do not want to know." Marius' playful smile was back. "Shall we walk?" He offered his arm.

I took it, but something bothered me. All that had been was simply a roundabout way of telling me that he had stolen it. That worried me quite a bit, but I couldn't quite decide what to do about it.

"Where are we going?" I asked, putting the conversation out of my mind, or at least trying.

"Well, dear lady, that is a surprise, and therefore you are not supposed to know."

"I am not sure if I like surprises or not," I confessed.

"Then now is a good time to find out. Do not worry, this will be fun. Very simple, local wonder and all that." He squeezed my arm a little. "Now, relax a bit." He looked at me. "You look like a queen with your beautiful long hair and the bracelet. It's just perfect for you."

"Thank you." I smiled happily. So what if Marius had stolen the bracelet? People stole trinkets all the time. Anyway, Marius might have been telling the truth. What proof did I have that his mother did not give it to him?

The lie that I was telling myself was as flimsy as the lie Marius had fabricated, but I couldn't bear to take my arm from his.

"Here we are." Marius stopped in front of a building. Sweet, warm scents wafted lazily from the door and open windows.

I looked up at the sign. It was the bakery. We walked inside.

"Sit down right there." Marius steered me towards a stool and slid his arm out of mine. "I am going to go and find the baker. He must be in the back room."

I slowly sat. The room was musty. All the tables and counters were dusted white with flour.

Marius was only gone for a few moments. He came back with a man who fulfilled every aspect of what I had always imagined a baker to look like. He was of medium height, and a heavy build. His eyes were a dark navy blue, and so round and large that they seemed to overshadow the rest of his features.

Except one thing, his rich, dark brown skin. I had never seen anything like it. I stood and extended my hand. The baker shook it. Though his hand enveloped mine, his grip was gentle and warm.

"My name is Daemon Rodaeo," the man said. His voice was low, thick, and sounded like music. "It is wonderful to meet you."

"Rapunzel. It is a pleasure to meet you too." I curtseyed, wobbling a bit.

"Daemon is from the plains in the East. He is the best baker in the kingdom." Marius slapped Daemon on the back. "Fit to bake for a king, I always say."

"Now that is a lie, my friend. You have always been fond of embellishing the truth. On one point, however, you are right. I am from Fyalid, one of the tribes in the eastern kingdoms. This is why my skin is so much darker than yours." He directed the last of this sentence towards me.

"Oh?" I had been afraid to ask for fear of insulting him.

"I could tell that you were wondering by the way that you were staring." He saw the panicked look on my face. "Do not worry. I am not offended. Many people in the town ask me many questions. If you were in my homeland, I would be the one staring at you." He laughed.

"Rapunzel, Daemon is going to show you his best pastry," Marius said eagerly.

"Show me? I don't get to eat it?" I asked.

"Oh, of course. What I meant is that you get to eat it, but first, you get to see it, and that is perhaps even better." Marius took my hand and pulled me to the counter.

Daemon, standing on the other side, pulled out a large lump of dough. He started to knead and flatten it. The dough squished methodically in between his fingers. Every so often he had to pick the dough off his hands.

"Why don't you use a rolling pin?" I asked. "It would be much easier and faster too, for that matter."

"Using our bare hands is a tradition. In my tribe, it is said that if we knead the dough with our hands, it infuses our soul into the bread. Anyone who eats it will be guaranteed a good, long life," Daemon said.

"Really? That actually works?" I asked.

"I am not sure. I just follow the tradition because I like the feeling of warm dough around my fingers," he admitted.

He seemed much happier working with the dough. After he had finished kneading it, he picked it up and folded it over on itself a few times. As he worked, he whistled a low haunting melody.

"Now, by doing this–" Daemon started, noticing me watching him intently.

"You are creating air bubbles in the dough, making it lighter." I finished for him.

"Well done. That is very good, Rapunzel."

Marius clapped a few times. "I didn't know that you cooked." He grabbed my hand. "I knew that you were full of surprises." He kissed the back of my fingers.

Next, Daemon started to spin the dough on his finger.

"This is where it gets exciting," Marius whispered, not wanting to disrupt Daemon's concentration. His breath in my ear did nothing to help *my* concentration, however. I lightly nudged him away.

The dough went round and round at Daemon's command. Without warning he started to toss it in the air. Flour spun in every direction. As he threw it, the dough fluctuated up and down, waving as it went.

"Toss me those strawberry slices. One at a time, now," Daemon said.

Marius picked up a bowl and started to pull out slices of strawberry. He threw the first one to Daemon.

The slice spun towards the dough. At the last moment, Daemon wrapped the dough around the incoming fruit.

"Marius, the least you could do is give me a little of a challenge," Daemon said.

Marius started to throw the strawberries a bit off course. Daemon still caught each piece in the dough. When the strawberries ran out, Marius grabbed a bowl of apple slices.

"And now, it is your turn Rapunzel." Marius handed the bowl to me.

"What? Me?" I asked.

"It's easy. Just throw it toward the dough. Daemon will get it no matter what," said Marius. When I didn't grab one, he placed a slice in my hand. "Throw it."

I flipped the apple slice. When it was swallowed but the dough, I shouted in glee. "Yes!" I cheered. "I did it!"

Both Daemon and Marius laughed. People seemed to like to laugh at me.

I let the rest of the apple slices go flying. All of them ended up in the dough.

Daemon let the dough rest in his hands. It was spotted with strawberries and apples. He rolled it into a long snake shape. When it was about a foot long, he twisted it around itself. Daemon stuck it into the oven. I caught sight of the flames as the baker opened and closed the tall metal door.

"It will take only about twenty-five minutes to cook properly. In fifteen, I will take it out to sprinkle it with some spices." Daemon wiped off his hands. White was dusted over his face.

"You only made one. What about me?" Marius asked.

"I only made enough dough for one, and the lady gets first priority. Is that a problem for you?" Daemon took a rag and rubbed it over the flour-covered counter. It didn't do much but spread the white powder.

"Nah, I suppose not. I've got too many other things to worry about," Marius said, looking around.

"Yes, I heard about that." Daemon lowered his voice a bit. "Have the guards stopped bothering you yet?" The both of them glanced furtively my way and leaned closer together.

"You know, I really do have excellent hearing. Whispering is only making you look foolish. Why are you hiding from the guards?" I asked.

The two looked at each other again and reluctantly moved away. "It was just a little misunderstanding with a pair of shoes, that's all." Marius waved the matter away.

"Shoes? I heard that it was a horse." Daemon gave Marius a long stare.

"Did you?" Marius looked a little shaken. "It is hard to keep these things straight, you know."

Daemon stared at Marius for another moment, and then turned his attention to me. "Rapunzel, why don't you tell me about yourself?" Daemon took a seat on the other side of Marius.

"That is a lovely idea," Marius said. "When it comes down to it, I just realized that I don't know as much about you as I would like."

"True. If we are going to change the topic of conversation, it ought to be a good one, right?" I said.

Daemon whistled. "My dear girl, nothing throws you, does it? You are not affected by Marius' tricks. Who taught you that?"

I was taken aback by the compliment. At least, I thought that it was a compliment. I wasn't quite sure what his words meant. "My mother taught me. Actually, she is not my mother, but she is as good a mother as I will ever have, though. Talking to people like this is a rare occurrence for me, so I suppose that I take care to pay proper attention to what someone is saying." Did I really just say that? I was sounding like a simpleton in front of Marius.

"Where do you live? Obviously not in Acada, but close enough to visit often, I suppose." Marius leaned in, interested.

"Oh, we live in a small cottage in the woods. My adoptive mother Jacqueline enjoys solitude. I don't get out much."

Marius looked shocked. I could not quite tell what had made him react the way he did, but I guessed that it was when I mentioned Jacqueline's name. It was as if he were putting two and two together. He didn't rejoin the conversation until Daemon commented on my hair.

"Going on looks alone, I would have said that she was a princess, but do not be fooled. Deep down inside, she is really just another country bumpkin," said Marius as he rubbed my head.

"Stop it," I said. When he refused, I lightly swatted his hand away.

Daemon shook his head at us, a smile dancing on his lips, and opened the oven. He took out the partly-cooked pastry and sprinkled some brown dust on it.

"I do hope that you enjoy cinnamon, Miss Rapunzel," Daemon said as he pinched some into the dough.

"Oh yes. It has been so long since I had any." My mouth watered at even the faintest whiff of the spice.

"Today is your lucky day then." Marius smiled.

Daemon stuck the roll back into the oven, but the scent lingered in the air even after it was out of sight.

"What do you do with your time?" Daemon asked. "What do you like?"

"I sing," I offered, hoping desperately that neither Marius nor Daemon would ask the question that was sure to follow.

"Sing for us," said Marius. It was more of a command than a question.

"Oh no, I couldn't." I looked imploringly at Daemon.

"Go on, we both beg of you," Daemon said.

I sighed and searched my thoughts. I had the perfect song. It was the story of a baker who left his home in search of legendary flour which created bread that came to life.

Jacqueline often sang it to me when we cooked dinner together.

Daemon and Marius were the perfect audience. They laughed when they should have and were silent when they needed to be. When I had finished, they both stood and clapped.

"Bravo, Rapunzel. Why didn't you tell me before that you were one of the lucky few with a voice like an angel?" Marius asked.

"I'm not that good. Daemon's right, you're just a horrible exaggerator," I accused.

"I would never lie about something as important as this." Marius crossed his heart in a solemn promise.

"Yes, you would. You are shameless." I jabbed my finger into his chest.

"Oh, really? Then I guess that it wouldn't be a surprise if I did this." He lunged at me, caught me around the stomach and began to tickle me mercilessly.

"Stop it! Marius!" I screamed, laughing uncontrollably.

"Break it up, you two. No tomfoolery in my establishment," Daemon said, not seeming terribly concerned. He peeked into the oven. "Your roll is done, Rapunzel."

For a moment, all that registered in my mind was the heavenly smell drifting from the large pastry Daemon held up. I relaxed in Marius' grip.

"What is it called?" I asked, inhaling, my eyes squeezed tightly shut so that I could focus solely on the aroma.

"Just a roll. It is new and so I have not named it yet. Have any ideas?" Daemon asked.

"I was thinking: Dariun," Marius said. "Just imagine. A customer walks in and you say 'can I help you?' They'll walk up to the counter and say, 'yes. I will have two Dariuns please.'" Marius glanced at me, raising his eyebrows a few times, dark eyes twinkling.

"Dariun? That's awful," I said through my laughter.

"No, it's great. Our names put together, the creators of the masterpiece."

"First of all, that is without a doubt, the most dreadful name I have ever heard. And second, you helped make this? Somehow, you don't seem like someone who knows a tablespoon from a teapot," I said.

"There's a difference?" he asked. When I raised an eyebrow he grudgingly conceded. "Fine, I don't know anything about cooking, but my mere presence was an inspiration to Daemon."

"Really? I seem to remember you running off after I kicked you out of the kitchen. I do not recall seeing you after that," Daemon said, winking at me.

"Fine! I got out of the way, that's how I helped, but it was a big help."

Daemon rolled his eyes behind Marius' back. "Shut your mouth, boy. Let the poor girl eat." He wrapped the roll up in a cloth and handed it to me. "You best be going now. I have got to prepare some more dough," the baker said.

"Thank you so very much," I said, pulling the wrapped roll close to me.

"Come back anytime. My doors are always open to you." Daemon disappeared into a back room.

Marius and I left. I put my arm through his and let him lead. I didn't pay attention to where we were going, but rather started to eat my deliciously warm pasty.

"Where would you like to go?" Marius asked.

I shrugged vaguely. My mouth was too full of dough to answer coherently.

"Hmm, where to go…" Marius snapped his fingers. "I know! Come, we are about to journey to the heart of our pleasant little town."

We veered off the path we had been on and pushed through an increasingly dense crowd of people.

It wasn't until my roll was completely gone that I bothered to look up. We were in the marketplace where Marius had first bumped into me. Once more it was overflowing with people.

"This time, I will try hard to not knock you over. How would you like to have a proper tour?" Marius asked enthusiastically.

I smiled. "I would love a tour."

We headed over to a tall, lanky man selling jewelry. He had rings in his ears and nose. His large Adam's apple stuck out in comparison to his long thin neck.

"Rapunzel, this is Philip, my very closest associate." Marius gestured smoothly toward Philip. "Philip, Rapunzel is a new friend. She is visiting the town today. I am her chaperone, for the moment anyway. I have no doubt that her dreadful friend Sven will be along any minute."

Philip nodded his head and I took my lead from him, nodding shortly in return.

"Philip has some of the finest jewelry around. He imports the pieces from six different countries," Marius informed me.

"Yes. Seven if you count Nago." Philip looked bored; he fiddled with a bit of dirt under his fingernail.

"Nobody counts Nago, it's far too small. It is a good place to hide, though. Philip is my most trusted friend. We count on each other for everything," Marius said proudly.

I avoided Philip's eyes. I did not like something about him. His eyes shifted too much to be a good man. The fact that he was friends with Marius, who I liked but wasn't quite sure I trusted, didn't help either.

"May I look?" I asked, stepping closer to his wares.

"I don't mind, but do not break or even touch for that matter," Philip said harshly.

I wrinkled my nose at him and bent over the jewels. The temptation to pick them up was almost more than I could bear. There were necklaces, bracelets, rings for a person to put in their nose or ears, rings to go on the fingers. They were made up of anything and everything: metal, glass, and even cloth. My hands hovered over it all, trying to keep my promise not to touch.

Philip frowned at my left wrist, the one with Marius' bracelet on it.

"Wait a moment, isn't that mine?" he asked suspiciously.

"No, of course not!" Marius said hurriedly, pulling me away and effectively hiding my wrist. We left Philip's wares in a rush. Marius said that it was because Philip didn't like people to linger, but I saw the look in his eyes.

We met with many more people. With each of them, Marius claimed that they were his "most trusted associate." I wondered who the one he actually trusted most was. Most likely it was none of them. I liked the men well enough; they were charming and I had a hard time imagining them being thieves. I pretended that these men weren't criminals at all, just real businessmen, but I knew that it wasn't true. They were still kind, though a few of them made me nervous.

Yes, the men were nice enough; it was the women I distrusted. When we encountered any females, young or old, Marius would sweep over, kiss their cheeks and ask gallantly how they were. Each woman blushed and said they were well. It was obvious that this was a routine for him. I knew that I was being petty, but I didn't appreciate sharing the attention.

Eager to get away from these women, I said, "I need to go to the stables. Will you come with me?" I looked at the cobblestones, searching for the black ones intermixed with the light. I spotted them and started off to the right.

"It is this way, Rapunzel." Marius steered me to the left instead. "This will be much faster."

"This is why people don't leave me alone," I said. At least we had left the others behind. I had Marius' complete attention again.

"Now, why are we going to the stables?" Marius asked nonchalantly, as we passed through the crowd of people.

"Sven and I are meeting up," I said.

Marius let go of my hand. I had not even realized that he was holding it. "Oh, I see. I don't want to intrude the two of you."

"It is not like that," I said quickly. "We're just friends."

"Friends who meet alone in the stables? I don't think so." Marius moved away.

"It's not like that," I repeated.

"Really? Then enlighten me," he said, suddenly agitated.

"We are looking for someone. He went missing a few weeks ago. His name is William, and he is Sven's best friend. We have to find him soon." I grabbed his shoulder to prevent him from going.

"Well then I am coming with you." Marius stopped trying to get away.

I kept going towards the stables, but I shot Marius a glance. "No, you're not. You have got to stay here."

"I'm confused. At first you wanted me to come with you, and now I'm supposed to stay here?" Marius followed me. "Pick one or the other."

I sputtered a bit. Marius' words mixed me up. Which one did I want?

"Listen, is it going to be dangerous?" Marius asked.

"Oh, possibly." Perhaps I could dissuade him from coming.

"There will be wolves, I assume."

"Wolves?" The image of a large wolf foaming at the mouth came to my mind. I did not like that idea at all.

"Yes, the woods are swarming with them this time of year," Marius said as we entered the stables.

"Swarming?" I repeated.

"Wolves, snakes, bears, you name it, and the woods have it. They're a death trap waiting to happen." Marius leaned up against a wall. "Wild animals have habit of grouping together and attacking people in groups of two or less." He waved his hand. "But don't worry. I'm sure that you and Sven will be fine. I already know that he won't hesitate to use his sword."

Sven walked in then. "Oh," he said when he saw Marius. "It's you. What is he doing here?" he asked me.

"We were– I was telling–" I couldn't decide what to say. "I was thinking that maybe we need another person in our group," I said. He stared at me. I added, "You know, to keep away the wolves."

"No, I don't think so," Sven said firmly.

"What if we get lost? Two are more likely to get lost than three."

"I just bought a compass and a better map. They are worth at least one person each, which means our group, ever increasing, has grown to four. Surely we won't get lost now." Sven spun me around. "Now go find Resa."

"Did you hear what I said about wolves? Three people are much safer than two, and that's a fact," I said over my shoulder.

Sven spun me again and looked me right in the eyes. There was no way he could miss the terror I felt.

"Wolves, huh?" Sven asked. "And this guy's going to protect us?" I shrugged and nodded. "All right. Get a horse, Marius."

"Oh, I am flattered. I did not think that you would remember me at all, let alone my name," Marius said.

I thought it best that I not leave the two alone for long, so I ran off quickly to go get Resa, but I heard Sven and Marius talking as I left.

"You know that there are no wolves in these forests, right?" Sven asked.

"Oh, I know," Marius said.

"Just making sure." Sven seemed to let the subject go.

I smiled. That sly man had lied. There were no wolves and he knew it. I should have suspected that Marius would pull such a trick.

Another thought came to my mind. I was about to go traversing into the woods with Sven and Marius. How long we would be gone was unknown. Was there anyway that the two could get along for time enough to find William?

CHAPTER FOURTEEN

"You sure that you're leading us the right way?"

"Positive. Let me do this my way. Go steal something. Leave me alone."

Sven and Marius had been arguing like this for hours. Sven would not let Marius get near the maps, determined to navigate without the thief's help. Marius would not let up badgering Sven. Both believed themselves to be in the right. Arguments got louder and more heated. Fists were about to start flying.

It was getting dark and I was sick of their antics. We had to be close to a town, but the men couldn't decide which way it was.

"Give me the map," I said, squeezing Resa between Bruce and Strider, Marius' horse.

"What?" Marius and Sven asked together, stopping their arguments for the first time since we had set out.

"Just hand me the map." I held out my hand, but when Sven didn't give it over, I snatched it. With a snap, I set it in front of me and smoothed it out. I examined it carefully and handed it back. With a flick of my reins, I started in a new direction, not too far off of where we had been going.

Both of their mouths moved wordlessly for a few moments. Their horses stopped, but it took me a few seconds to realize that they were not following me.

"It's this way, in case you were wondering. You were both wrong." I nodded in the direction of the town.

The men looked at each other.

"You always seem to be saying that she is your responsibility. Don't look at me that way," Marius said, looking over at Sven.

"You're a bad influence. It's not my fault."

The two stopped arguing for a bit, though I did see them cast angry looks out of the corners of their eyes.

As we walked, I asked Sven if I could see his dagger. At first he refused, claiming to not trust me with sharp objects, but he finally handed it over with a stern warning not to poke anyone's eye out.

"I'm not a complete idiot. I can hold a knife without hurting anyone," I said, turning it over and over in my hands. It glittered softly.

"It's a dagger, not a knife," Sven said softly to himself.

I didn't respond. Sven definitely underestimated my ability with the weapon. I had been practicing at home. It was only a few minutes later that I saw my opportunity to prove him wrong. I threw the dagger; it whizzed past Sven's head, he yelled and ducked.

"What was that for?" he shouted.

I didn't have to answer. Marius did so for me.

"Holy," he interjected with some words I had never heard. "Look at that." He pointed to where my knife was.

I smiled smugly when Sven caught sight of the snake pinned to a tree by the weapon. I had seen it wrapped around a branch right behind Sven.

It was a Vipera berus, a common adder. I was surprised that it had been rising up to strike Sven because adders didn't usually bite unless they were provoked. *Jacqueline can control snakes.* A voice said in my mind, but I dismissed it. Jacqueline didn't know that I was gone. She was on a trip. She had told me that she wouldn't be back for days, so there was no way she had sent the snake.

"What was that you were saying earlier about me not needing to be able to use this?" I asked Sven.

Sven's mouth moved, but no words came out. He was pale as ice as he turned to look at me. "It could've–" He stopped. He knew what an adder bite was like. Several people had been bitten in the village. One had died, but although the rest had lived, they were in terrible pain for anywhere from six months to a year.

We reached the large town of Tia as the sun disappeared behind the far away mountains. Luckily, one of the first buildings we found was an inn.

I let Sven and Marius talk to the innkeeper. As soon as they had the keys, I ran to my room and locked the door behind me.

As I put my hair down, I sighed, my back to the door. I couldn't walk one more step, and so falling to my knees, I crawled to the bed and burrowed under the covers. I felt as if I were back in the tower, it was a comfortable feeling.

An incessant knocking woke me in the morning. It grew louder and louder as I ignored it.

"Go away," I told my pillow, eyes shut tight. "I'm never coming out. I am going to sleep in this wonderful bed forever."

"Come on, it's time for breakfast," Sven called through the door.

"No. I'll just starve." The bed was oh-so-warm.

"She's not going to come out. I'm going in," Marius said. "Let me just pick this lock."

Thwap. "Get away from the door. She's a lady. You don't go bursting through a lady's bedroom door." Sven must have hit Marius. "Rapunzel, you're not going to get to eat if you don't come out."

I groaned. It seemed far too early for the sun to have woken up, let alone to be time to eat. But Sven knew my weakness. I could not turn down food.

Unable to muster the energy to stand or even sit up, I rocked back and forth until I had enough momentum to roll out of bed. I hit the floor hard, but the wood had been warmed by the sun and I was not uncomfortable.

It took me only ten minutes to get ready and head to the dining room, for once I was out of bed I found that I was extremely hungry.

There were sausages, eggs, pancakes, all the dishes a person would expect to see at a breakfast table. For a moment I thought that I had died. It was far too appetizing.

"Well that took you long enough," Marius remarked, halfway through a pancake.

I sat down in between him and Sven, but before I could shoot back a snide remark, a woman came up to Marius and hit the back of his head with a stack of papers.

"Marius! I didn't ever imagine that you would be in my neck of the woods again!" she cried, putting her hands on her hips.

Marius spun, his face lighting up when he saw the woman.

"Valerie?" he exclaimed, a smile forming on his lips. "I completely forgot that this is where you settled down." The smile broke out into a fully-formed grin. "Lucky town, to be the one to finally claim you."

"Marius! You never paid me back, you–" Out of Valerie's mouth spouted words that Jacqueline had never said, but I had read in a few of my shadier books.

"Calm down there, lass. I've got your money." Marius patted his pocket subconsciously. He turned to me. "Rapunzel, I want you to meet Valerie, my–"

"Yes, I know. You're closest associate," I said, finishing the sentence for him.

"His closest associate? Dear me, does he really still say that? No. He owes me money. He skipped out on me about two years ago. I never thought that I was going to get my coins back."

"Oh ye of little faith. You'll get your money back; never you worry. More importantly, I have someone for you to meet. Valerie, Rapunzel is a newly met friend of mine. We're working on a very important task. One of those jobs, if you know what I'm talking about." Marius winked at her. He glanced at Sven out of the corner of his eye. "Oh, and this is Sven, her friend," he added quickly.

"A pleasure to meet you both." Valerie curtseyed prettily, getting much lower than I could have managed.

"Have you worked in the palace, Miss Valerie?" Sven asked. I looked over at him. How could he know that? Did he know her? If so, she would be bound to remember his face or his name. Perhaps she would recognize him.

"Why, that is right." Valerie looked impressed. "Years and years ago. That is quite impressive. But it's not Miss." She held out her left hand, where lay a golden wedding band.

"Married? For how long? Why did I not know?" Marius asked, annoyed. He stood and grabbed Valerie's hand to examine the ring.

"One year and three weeks, if you are going to be exact." Valerie didn't pull her hand away. She seemed to enjoy the attention. "You were not invited to the wedding because I didn't want you to ruin the ceremony, whether accidentally or on purpose."

"Ruin it? You think that I would ruin your ceremony? Never. I'm great at parties, you know that," Marius said defensively.

Valerie looked at him carefully. "Is that so? I could probably find at least one person in every town in the nearest thirty miles who would swear differently.

"Eh. People don't know everything. Honestly, many people don't know anything." Marius said.

"You have not lost your insulting sense of humor, I see." Valerie thought for a moment. "I have an idea. There is a celebration today; there will be dancing later on. Why don't you all come? It would be a chance for you to relax for a day, enjoy the town. You could meet my husband, Giles." None of us answered right away, so she kept going. "It would be so much fun. I could find a dress for Rapunzel, and I am sure that Giles would have some suits that would fit both Sven and you, Marius."

"Well," Marius said, obviously pretending to think about it. "I don't know, a night of dancing and free food? That's a tough one. What do you think, Rapunzel?" He turned to me.

"It sounds like a fun time to me. I've never been to a dance before. I would like to go." I turned to Sven. "What do you think? I am sure that you have been to dances such as this many times before. Would you prefer not to go?"

"We are running out of time," he started. I tried to keep the begging look off of my face and failed. "But I think that we should go. I mean, how often are you going to be able to go to a dance here? Yes. We will take one day's leave. Tomorrow, we will leave to go resume our search. Until then, I suggest we enjoy ourselves."

"Oh, Sven! Thank you so much! We will search from dawn until dusk." I saw that he was faking the smile on his face. I leaned in and said in his ear, "We will find him, I promise. Maybe you'll even pick up some hints of where he may be. You will see, and I will be right. Have faith. This is not over yet."

"Yes, I suppose that you are right," he muttered back with a sigh.

I leaned away and smiled broadly. "Now come. Let us accept Valerie's offer with the grace and dignity that it merits," I said.

Valerie joined my smile. "You two finish your breakfast." She grabbed Marius' arm. "We have some money issues to look over. Rapunzel, I will be back to get you and help you get ready in one hour. What room are you staying in?"

"Thirteen."

"One hour, then you let me take over," she said. "Sven, you and Marius are going to be given clothes to borrow. When we are done talking, go with him to Churl Road."

Valerie left, dragging Marius behind her. I looked at Sven. He was eating contentedly as if nothing had happened.

"Come on. You must do this all the time, you will be the best dancer," I said.

"Yes, I do this all the time that is true. I also fail at this all the time. I am terrible at dances." He continued to eat.

"Can you dance?" I asked.

"Oh yes, I suppose, I took all of the lessons, practiced for hours, read the books, everything that a prince is expected to do," he said, rolling his eyes.

"Then I don't understand the problem."

"I simply can't enjoy the dance itself. Halfway through, I start to yawn. There is nothing enjoyable for me. Why would I care to stand for hours on end, if only to be gawked at by girls and women who enjoy the sight of my crown more than they do my face?" He stabbed the sausage with his fork savagely, trying to appear interested in his food, and unhurt by the thought.

"That's all?"

"What do you mean, that's all? Is that not enough?" Sven asked loudly. "You try being interested in the lives of every dignitary who comes to visit. Honestly, they are not that exciting."

"No, I'm sorry, that is not what I meant. What I meant to say was that you don't have to worry about that," I said.

"Oh? And why is that?" Sven asked, finally pushing his plate away.

"No one knows that you are the prince. If you play this right, you can go all day without anyone getting suspicious. Unless you ruin everything by talking to Valerie."

"How would I ruin everything?"

"How did you know that she worked in the palace?"

"That was easy. Her curtsey. All the maids have to learn to curtsey that low. There was a ninety percent chance that I was right, and I took it."

"She was definitely getting suspicious. You have to remember that you cannot act as you normally do."

Sven stood, ready to leave. "I can do that." He shivered a bit, excited.

"Geez, you're like a little kid." I stood too and left for my room

It could not have been a half hour before Valerie showed up. Her smile was brighter, and I could have sworn that her purse was just a bit bigger.

"I know that I am a bit early, but we have so little time," she said.

"But isn't the party not until tonight?" I asked.

"Oh, heavens no! I don't know how they do things where you are from, but here, we celebrate only a few days a year, and the festivities last from noon to midnight." She walked with me from my room and out of the inn.

When we got outside, I stopped briefly. It was so warm. I still had bare feet and the cobblestones felt nice beneath my toes. Then I finally understood what Valerie had said.

"Wait a moment. Noon to midnight? We have to dance for twelve hours?" I couldn't imagine standing still for that long, let alone dancing.

"No, the dancing does not start until seven o'clock. Out in the square, shops give out free food, there is celebrating, bands are playing, the Governor comes out and listens to anyone's questions, and the roaming players stop by and perform." Valerie sighed. "You are very lucky to have stopped in town for today."

"Yes, I suppose."

Valerie raised her hand and a carriage stopped in front of us. We climbed in and the driver nodded at Valerie.

"Ah, Mrs. Schultz, do you wish to be dropped off at your home?" he asked.

"Yes, thank you" Valerie affirmed.

"Whatever you say, Mrs. Schultz." The driver turned back to the road.

This kind of transportation seemed to be what Valerie was used to. I supposed that she had quite a bit of money. The carriage ride was longer than I had expected, and when we got out, we had almost left the town entirely. In front of us sat an enormous manner. I gaped at the size of it. Valerie saw me and smiled proudly.

"Four floors, two grand staircases, two kitchens and ten bedrooms, not including the master bedroom Giles and I share." She left the packages in the carriage. I started to pick them up. "Oh don't bother, Rapunzel, the servants will bring them in."

"Your house is beautiful," I said, trying not to act like the country bumpkin Marius had called me.

"Thank you. Wait until you see the inside," said Valerie as she opened the door.

The house was even more stunning inside. Acting as the gracious hostess, Valerie gave me a complete tour. We stopped in her room and stepped into her dressing room.

As we walked in, my jaw dropped. I had never imagined so many dresses could exist in the entire world, let alone fit in one room. It was a bit horrifying.

"What color, do you think?" Valerie asked.

"I have no idea." I followed her around like a puppy.

"I think that maybe a nice green to match your eyes would be nice. What do you think about that?"

"Uhh…"

"Would you rather that I pick your dress out for you?" Valerie asked kindly.

I breathed a sigh of relief. "Oh, thank you. I've never been much good with clothing. It always made Jacqueline crazy that I didn't care what I wore."

"Who is Jacqueline?"

"She is the woman who took me in after my mother died. She thought that it was very important for me to look my best, but there were never many people to look nice for." I reached out hesitantly to feel the cloth of some of the dresses. They were so soft.

"You have met the right person then. People come to me for their troubles in clothing." She turned away and began to sift through the racks of dresses.

Trying not to roll my eyes, I sat on a small chair at one end of the store. It was not quite large enough to be comfortable and I wondered at the purpose of it.

"This is gorgeous. Look at this, Rapunzel." Valerie held out a dress. I saw that it was green, but I paid little attention.

"Yes, you're right," I said distractedly.

"Rapunzel, I'm not stupid. You didn't even look at it. Just go over there and put it on." Valerie shoved the dress at me and pushed me to the right towards a shade to change behind.

I went behind it, pulled the edge to the wall, undressed and slowly slipped into the large dress. It was a pretty color; a light green that matched the grass and my eyes. There was no mirror, however, and I could not see what it looked like.

I walked carefully to Valerie, holding the dress at my shoulders. It wouldn't stay up alone until she tied the back.

"I see that you don't wear a corset," said Valerie as she laced my dress. "Lucky girl. They're useless creations. Except for this night, however. You will wear one, and you will thank me." She sighed. "You're a beautiful girl, Rapunzel."

"Thank you. I have got to mention though, you are also very lovely." I glanced at her out of the corner of my eye.

"Yes, but I am much stouter. Now stop squirming so I can tie this properly."

I tried to stay still as a statue. My breath cut off for a moment when Valerie pulled each row tight. I was not sure if I was going to be able to dance.

The dress laced up from the lowest part of my back, and so it took a few minutes for Valerie to finish.

"Turn around in a circle," Valerie said, motioning with her finger.

I did as she said. Valerie clasped her hands together. "You are stunning. This is the one."

I went back behind the shade and changed into my everyday dress. I shouldered my pack filled with my hair. I had taken it off when I tried on the dress, but had put it by my feet and left my hair wrapped in it. Though she must have wondered, Valerie had not commented on it as of yet.

After she had carefully folded the dress and put it aside, she steered me over to rows and rows of shoes. I glanced down at my bare feet.

Valerie followed my gaze, saw my feet and gaped, "Did you lose your shoes while we were walking? Where could they have gone?"

"I… I never had any shoes. I never needed any in the woods," I said, embarrassed.

"Marius never bought you any?" She asked, indignantly.

"Marius didn't notice, I suppose, and buying me shoes is not something that Sven would think of," I said.

"We are going to fix that right now. Shoes are easy.

Valerie picked up a pair of black shoes with small, thick heels. I could tell they were expensive. They were shiny, with fancy stitching and silk lacing. To my dismay, she held them out to me.

"Do you like these? They are not too high, so I figure that you'll be able to dance with them, even if you are not used to heels."

I sat on a stool and pulled the shoes on awkwardly. They did not feel good on my feet.

"I don't think they fit," I said, grimacing. Every second I wore the boots, my feet hurt a little more. I shifted restlessly from side to side.

Valerie covered her mouth with a hand. She was holding back a laugh. I could not quite figure out what was so amusing.

"What? Did I do something wrong?" I asked.

"Rapunzel, they are on the wrong feet," Valerie said through a laugh.

I blushed and switched them. Now my feet felt much better. I stood, carefully in case I lost my balance.

"Perfect fit. I am a genius, aren't I? Walk around a bit. Make sure that they don't hurt when you move about."

I did as she said. The feeling of shoes was awkward at first, because it had been so long since I had worn them. After the first few steps, however, my feet remembered how to adjust my walking when the shoes were on. They were not terribly uncomfortable.

"They are not too high, so I figure that you'll be able to dance with them, even if you are not used to heels," Valerie said absentmindedly. "Undoubtedly they will hurt a little after a while, but that is the price of beauty. As women, our job is to look nice, act complacent," She took the dance shoes from me and put them next to the dress. "And only when the men turn their backs do we put our intellect to good use."

The way Valerie described women disturbed me. I did not think that women should pretend to be docile when in public, but conniving as soon as the men stopped watching. I knew from reading books that women were normally not the dominant gender, but I did not plan on changing who I was for any man.

CHAPTER FIFTEEN

We made our way to the fitting room on the third floor. The fitting room was specifically for clothing to be adjusted. I wondered at the thought of living somewhere so large that you could devote an entire room to one task.

"There is a bath drawn for you. Go get clean. You look like you have been on the road for quite some time, and I'm sure that you would enjoy getting some of those layers of dirt off." Valerie pointed to a small room off to the left.

"That's very kind, but I don't feel layered in dirt. Do I look it?" I looked at myself. Was I really so filthy?

"No, you look fine, but as soon as you are clean, you will wonder at how you could stand being as you were for so long." She added as an afterthought, "Make sure you take your hair down and give it a good scrubbing."

I went into the room and found a bath waiting for me just as Valerie had promised. I folded my clothes and placed them in a corner. I pulled my hair all the way out of my bag but when I slipped into the tub, I left the braid hanging out the side. I didn't need to clean it. Jacqueline's potions made sure of that.

"Ahh," I sighed. The water was deliciously warm.

There was a bar of soap on a shelf nearby and I used it to scrub every inch of my body clear of dirt. I focused especially hard on my feet. It took a great deal of work, but I got all of the grime off. There was a towel on a chair that I used to dry myself off. When I was dried, I wrapped myself in a short robe. I went back into the fitting room, and Valerie smiled at how clean I was, but gasped when she saw my hair dragging behind me.

"Oh my goodness! I thought that it was unusually long, but I never imagined this," she exclaimed. "How far does it go?"

"Seventy feet or so," I said shyly.

"I did not think that hair could get that long in one lifetime." She came close and began to stroke it. "And it is so soft. How do you wash it?

"It's a spell that makes my hair grow abnormally fast and long. I don't need to wash it because the spell stops it from getting dirty," I explained.

Valerie whistled softly. "If only I could have hair this long. I have a million questions for you, but I don't think that I will ask any of them. I have never been fond of prying into other people's lives. I have my own secrets and I know that I would not appreciate it if people started wanting to know every detail of my life."

After Valerie had examined my hair for another few seconds, she sent me behind the screen to go put my dress on. A young pretty maid came to help me. Before she put on the dress, she picked up a corset.

"I'm Ava," she said as she tied the back.

"Rapunzel," I said, a little breathily as the fabric began to cut off my airflow. Inwardly I began to violently curse the person who invented these infernal pieces of clothing. It was probably a man.

After she finished with the corset and she had helped me into the dress, she had me go over to a stool in the middle of the floor and stand on it. I stretched my arms out the way she told me to and stood as still as I could.

"Can I have a mirror?" I was growing more and more curious about what I looked like.

"No, you may not. It will be so exciting when you look at yourself in the mirror for the first time, when you are completely finished, so no peeking until we're done with you," Valerie said sternly. She looked at Ava. "Just take her hem up a little, I think. Add a white sash, use whatever fabric you see fit." She smiled at me. "You are in good hands. Ava is the best seamstress around. I am going to go wash up. I do not think that I will see you until we are almost ready." Valerie left quickly.

"She's very excited about this festival. She has always been enthusiastic, but never like this. I think it is because Mr. Schultz won the election again, by a long shot too. He's become one of the most popular men in town," Ava said as she began to pin the dress up.

"Wait a moment, what election?" I asked.

"Governor, of course. Her husband is the governor of Tia," Ava said matter-of-factly.

That explained a lot. Why Valerie had so much money, why she had such a large house. I wondered for a moment why she hadn't told me. She was probably waiting until we met Giles, so that we could be surprised. I would not tell her that I knew.

Ava finished pinning the dress and got out her needle. She threaded it and brought it up to the dress, positioning it where she was going to begin.

"Don't I have to take it off before you can sew?" I asked. I had always thought that was how it worked. That's how Jacqueline did it.

"I was taught specifically to be able to sew clothing while it was still on the person. The Schultz family like things ready in a hurry, so all of the servants are trained to do things as fast as possible." Ava began to sew, carefully steering free of my legs so to not prick them with the needle.

"That takes great skill. The only time I can sew is when I am letting a hem out or fixing a minor tear." I wiggled a little and the needle bit me lightly. "Ouch."

"Sorry, you can't move or I'm bound to get you. Just stay still for five more minutes. I only have to take it up a half inch, and it's not taking long." Ava pulled the needle methodically in and out. "May I ask you a question?" she asked.

"I believe that you just did, but you are welcome to ask another," I said.

"Your hair, I heard you say that it was under a spell. I can tell that you don't want to talk about that, but I have to ask, is it heavy?"

"Sven once asked me that. I can't feel its weight. I suppose to others it's heavy, but I have to say no. I never even notice it." Another wiggle. Another stab.

"Stop it! You are going to be full of holes by the time I am done. Can you not be still?" Ava asked, exasperated. "You are making my hem go all funny."

BONG. BONG. BONG. An ear-splitting bell started to ring out. Twelve rings sounded before everything was still.

"Noon. The festivities are going to be starting now. I'll be swift. I have still got to go get my dress on. Mrs. Schultz gave all of the servants the day off as soon as they are done helping you and her get ready." Ava tied off the last knot and cut the thread with her teeth. "There you go. You're beautiful. If you would go sit at that table in the corner, Melody will be in to figure out what to do with that hair." Ava straightened. "Goodbye, Rapunzel, it was very nice to meet you, as brief as our meeting was." She left as quietly as she had entered. I could never be a servant here. I walked like an elephant.

I sat where I had been told and soon a different woman entered. She was short with cropped black hair and light brown eyes.

"Are you Melody?" I asked.

"Yes, and may I say, this is going to be quite a challenge. A wonderful experiment though. Finally, a chance to try all of the styles that I had never been able to do," she said with a combination of happiness at my hair and sadness at the townspeople's short hair.

"Why don't you grow your own hair?" I asked.

"I never do my own hair. I get my pleasure from seeing others all prettied up," Melody said. She added under her breath, "I think that first thing to do it call in some help." She rang a bell attached to the wall.

About four minutes later, two more women came rushing into the room. They stopped when they saw my hair.

Melody did not bother to introduce them. She snapped her fingers. "Grab a comb and help me straighten this out." She immediately started to undo the braid.

The put the brushes to my hair and started to stroke. I tried not to scream as knots were pulled out by their rough movements. Jacqueline had always been much gentler. I supposed that though the potion protected my hair from dirt, there was nothing to prevent it from tangling around itself. After ten minutes of intense pain, my hair began to feel smooth. I had forgotten the wonderful feeling of someone combing out my hair. I would never ever admit it out loud, but I enjoyed being taken care of.

As they brushed, Melody and her two helpers gossiped about things going on in the town. Melody gave hints on all the new hairstyles everyone would have. The redheaded woman spoke in sighs about the foods they would get to eat, most of them for free. The woman with blonde hair almost as white as milk was silent for a while before she mentioned the men that were coming.

"What about that man, Marius?" she asked me. "He is quite handsome, don't you think?"

"Penny!" cried the redheaded woman. "You know what Mrs. Schultz always says. Do not pry into the private affairs of the guests."

"Beth, you big worrywart. It does not hurt anybody to ask a simple question. She doesn't have to answer." She turned to me. "You don't have to answer that."

It took me a moment to respond. Penny was the blonde, Beth the redhead. At least now I knew their names. "He is very handsome," I said, praying that I was not blushing.

"There is not a girl in this town who doesn't know his name." Penny sighed. "Marius. You know, he's been on trial here four times for thievery. I think that it is so romantic." Another girlish sigh. I stared at her. Did I act like that? Heaven forbid.

"Did I hear my name?" a voice asked, coming from the hall outside the room. Marius poked his head in.

Penny and Beth squeaked in fright. Melody stood and motioned for him to leave. "Mrs. Schultz asked specifically for us to keep you away. Now, get!" When Marius didn't immediately disappear, Melody whacked him with the brush in her hand.

"Ow! I'm going, I'm going!" He was gone.

I heard laughing. That must have been Sven.

As soon as the men's footsteps faded, Penny looked at me slyly. "I did not know that there was another man with you. What is his name?" she asked.

I told them all about Sven. They oohed and ahhed in all the right places as I carefully shared a few of our adventures.

"You are so lucky," Beth said as she ran the brush though my hair.

I did not always think so.

"Beth, Penny, I think that we are done brushing. Now to get to work, I have an idea. Just stand by and hand me anything I ask for." Melody came right up to me and studied my head. "Rapunzel, I need you to cooperate."

I decided that Melody had magic fingers. First thing, she pulled my hair up into a ponytail on the very top of my head. I had not had my hair like that in a long time. She braided about four or five feet very tightly, wetting it occasionally to keep it in place. Once she was satisfied with the braid, she wound it around the top of my head. She pinned and knotted it to keep it in place and began to braid the rest. This second section of braid was looser to save time, but it was still more orderly than anything I had been able to do. The entire length of my hair was knotted this way.

"Stand up," Melody ordered. I did so. Melody wrapped her fingers around the braid that came out of the knot of hair on the top of my head and began to slide her hand down the braid. When she reached where my hair hit the floor, she backed up two inches and pulled the rest of my hair up. When it reached the knot, she pinned it up. She repeated this several times until she only had a few inches left. The result was many strands of braided hair going up and down my back many times, just missing the floor. The end she tucked into the hair on top so it disappeared.

"I'm finished," she said in satisfaction.

I wished more than ever for a mirror as Beth and Penny exclaimed about how beautiful I was.

"One more thing," Penny said. She reached into a drawer and pulled out some ribbon, whiter than her hair and almost as white as snow. With deft, practiced fingers, Penny threaded the ribbon through my hair.

"Go get your shoes, Mrs. Schultz will be coming in any minute," Melody said.

I did so and put them on just as Valerie swept through the door. She was glowing. Her black hair and red dress made her look mysterious and alluring. I could just imagine every man craning his neck to get a look at her. The dress hit quite low on her chest, but I was not going to critique her.

"Rapunzel, you are radiant!" She spun to Melody, Penny, and Beth. "You three work wonders. Go, get ready and leave for the festival whenever you wish. You are excused until tomorrow."

The three curtseyed and left in a hurry.

"Are you ready to see yourself?" Valerie asked me.

"I think so," I stammered. I was almost afraid to look. What if I did not like the dress or the way my hair was done?

"Come this way," she said, guiding me to the opposite end of the room. She pulled a sheet off of a large full-sized mirror.

I squeezed my eyes shut for a moment.

"Open those eyes," Valerie reproved.

In the mirror stared back a tall, elegant woman I did not know. She had hair like gold that folded up and down to the floor many times and knotted itself on the top of her head. The green dress was simple, with a wide white sash and embroidery only at the bottom, towards the hem. The dress matched her eyes, which were wide and a little wary. I could not believe that this woman was I.

"Something is missing," Valerie said, troubled. "I know." She rushed into the room with the tub and came back with my bag. She reached in and brought out the bracelet Marius had brought. "Put this back on." When I did so, her frown did not disappear. "There is still something missing. I just cannot figure out what it could be."

I looked at myself in the mirror. The dress barely skimmed the floor just as my hair did.

"I know. It's the neckline," Valerie said.

I looked down. It hit six fingers beneath the hollow of my throat, which was quite a bit lower than I usually put up with, but it was not as low as Valerie's. I hoped that she would not want to lower it.

"There is no embroidery. That is why something is missing. You need a necklace. I don't know if I have anything that would fit." Valerie lapsed into thought.

I did have something that would go perfectly. I had packed Jacqueline's necklace. Why I had brought it, I still was not quite sure. Perhaps I did not want to leave Jacqueline completely behind. I reached into my bag and pulled the necklace out carefully.

"Oh, that is perfect." Valerie said.

She helped clasp it around my neck and stood back, satisfied.

"Is that everything?" I asked.

Valerie stopped and thought. "Do you know how to dance?"

"Of course I know how to dance," I said. "I didn't grow up in a town like this, but I asked Jacqueline how to dance, and she showed me all of the dances she knew. I know three different swings, a folk dance," I started to list off. "A ribbon dance."

Valerie waved her hand impatiently. "Yes, that's lovely, but do you know how to dance with a man?"

I stopped. "Dance with a man? Yes, many of the dances that I learned were with partners." Why was she asking?

"Rapunzel." Valerie said, putting her hands on my shoulders and looking at me with the hint of a smile. "I don't mean those dances. I mean when the musicians slow down the rhythm, and you and a special man get close. Your heart rate goes up and you know that there's something special about this one." She laughed a little.

"Oh, no. I suppose not," I said, feeling foolish.

She sighed and glanced at a clock nearby. "Well, it's getting late, so let me just give you this piece of advice: let the boy lead." She started for the door.

"That's it?" I asked. "Follow the boy?"

"What more do you want?" She didn't give me time to answer. "The boys are waiting downstairs for us, we had better go."

I nodded grudgingly and walked with her to the stairs. Before we started down, I leaned over to Valerie. "I don't know if I can make it down without falling," I whispered.

"Hold the railing. Remember, there are two good looking young men waiting to catch you should you tumble," she said.

As we descended, Sven and Marius came into sight. Both were in nice black suits. Marius' hair was actually somewhat tamed. Both smiled when they saw us.

"Let us go," Valerie said. "Giles is going to meet me there."

Both men seemed to step forward, but Marius was faster. He offered his arm and I took it. It seemed strange to me that the sun as still high in the sky and we were going to a party, but I was excited nonetheless.

I was going to have at least one day in my life when I did not have to worry about Jacqueline, or missing people, or being different. After tonight, if I had to, I would go and live the rest of my life in the tower. I just needed one night of freedom, and then I would give the rest of my days to Jacqueline. I could finally be the complacent daughter she wanted.

"Shall we?" Marius asked as we started down the road. "The carriage is not coming. The roads are closed for the entire twelve hours."

"Yes," I said, feeling only a bit foolish. "We shall."

242

CHAPTER SIXTEEN

The town square was full of far too many people. They hustled and bustled about, eating the free food, listening to the small, randomly placed bands playing in corners and alleys. In the very center of the square was a traveling band of players. I could not tell exactly what play it was that they were performing, but the people around watching were laughing heartily.

"Giles is around here somewhere. I am going to go find him. Come and visit us later." Valerie started to migrate away. "And do not forget to bring me some food!" she called as she left.

Marius, Sven, and I stopped. The crowd around us was ever-changing. I supposed that I could sit there all afternoon and never see the same face twice.

"All right, where are we going?" Marius asked. "I have never been to the festival here before, but I have participated in other towns, so I figure it can't be much different." He looked to Sven. "Any preferences?"

"No. I have been to my share of festivals and I am always the person who has to decide where to go, and at what time." He looked around.

"All right Rapunzel, that means that it is up to you. Where to first?" Marius asked.

I was too busy watching people to answer. The women were all in fancy dresses and the men wore nice clothes.

"What are you thinking about?" Sven asked.

"I'm glad that we are not the only ones who dress up." It was the first thing that came to mind. Marius and Sven probably thought me crazy. "I mean, I just thought that Valerie was perhaps getting a bit overenthusiastic, and…is it always like this?"

Marius laughed. "Yes. Three times a year, everyone spends a ridiculous amount of money on new things and food in order to forget the hardships of the average day."

Sven sighed. "Perhaps if the king was a wiser ruler, the people's lives would be better," he said.

"I don't appreciate any talk of heresy in the presence of a lady. You have no right to say anything against the royal family. Do you even know anything about them?" Marius said, his voice serious, although perhaps not fully.

"I am sure that I know much more than you do. I could give you a few lessons on heresy. I know that the king does not appreciate your stealing," Sven said.

"You think that you know better than me, you little nanny boy? I could tell you a few things..." Marius started.

As the two started to argue heatedly, I slipped away. There was no way that I was going to listen to the two have a battle of words to decide which of them was manlier. I could not quite decide what they were trying to prove.

I did not want to miss anything, so I closed my eyes and spun in a circle a few times. When I had opened my eyes, the landscapes seemed to have changed completely. I headed to what was in front of me at the moment. The first thing that I came to was the group of players performing in the play I had seen the audience laughing at.

Instantly, I understood what was so funny. There was a man onstage with a human's body, but the head of a fish. He hobbled around the stage, gasping for breath while the other characters either ran away in fear or chased after him.

I wished to stay, and so I pushed my way lightly through the crowd. Few people protested. Many of them were too busy talking to each other animatedly to pay me much attention.

Towards the front I found a seat. Looking around to make sure that no one was coming to claim it, I stole towards it. As I sat, I pulled my hair out of the way.

During the remaining half hour of the play, I laughed so hard that tears ran down my face relentlessly. At the end, when the fish-man finally broke the spell and regained his human head, everyone stood and clapped.

I wandered away, a new thought on my mind. Sven was cursed, but how? I had never thought to ask what the curse actually entailed. It was a foolish blunder on my part, considering that I had entrusted my life to him the moment I had gotten on his horse. I resolved to ask him about it when I met back up with him.

I stumbled across a small band playing with a wide circle around it. There were a few men dancing alone in the middle. I watched along with the crowd, enjoying the show.

"Here is a lovely lady. Will you dance with me, lady?" One of the men had come up to me.

"Oh, my. I–"

"Come on, it will be lots of fun." The man pulled me into the circle. As we started to dance, I was very glad that I had begged Jacqueline to teach me a few years ago. It wasn't one of the elegant pieces that Valerie had been speaking about, but I thought that I would not like those songs quite as much. We spun and hopped, the crowd cheering us on. The man spun me and suddenly I found myself holding hands and dancing with Marius instead.

"How?" I asked, as we danced.

Marius smiled mysteriously, but did not answer. He was a good dancer, keeping me on the beat when I faltered. He led very well, and I had no illusion about who was controlling the dance, something that bothered me, though I didn't know why.

When the song ended, he bowed and kissed my hand. The crowd cheered. I turned around to see Sven. He waited at the edge of the crowd, looking a little downtrodden.

"I told you that we would find her," Marius said. "Come on, Valerie will be expecting us to find her soon." He started off.

Sven and I followed behind. Sven shook his head at me.

"What? Did I do something wrong? I was not going to sit there all day and let you and Marius fight it out," I said, defensively.

"It's not that," he said. "It's just; whenever you slip away from me you manage to find him. Why is that?"

I didn't answer, and I didn't need to. Sven answered his own question.

"I'm sure that I could blame this one on the curse. It is mightily convenient how often I can blame things that go wrong on the curse."

"You talk about the curse, but you know, you have never actually told me what the curse is," I said. "Care to explain a little?"

Sven thought for a moment. "There's no simple way to describe it. The idea is that no one will ever trust me; no one will take me in. If that means that something tangible would have to happen to make people believe in magic, the curse will make it happen. At the village, animals would get sick around me, things would fall off the walls; I've gotten hit by quite a few pots. Crops often seemed to have a worse year if I were nearby. When I thought that I had a chance to break the curse, you and Jacqueline disappeared. A king adopted me, but I don't fit in. I went off to rescue my best friend, but

I got lost.... Need I go on?" He had a faraway look as we walked. "It is always when I think that I have finally found something right, that it all goes horribly wrong. Marius is what went horribly wrong." He shook his head and strode a little faster, forcing me to catch up. I wobbled dangerously in my heels.

Marius waited for us a little ways away with three mugs of mint tea. He smiled broadly as he handed a cup to me.

"It is one of my favorite drinks. You might have to pull me away from here, because I am tempted to sit here all day sipping tea," Marius laughed as we sat down at a table.

I nodded, but my mind was still dwelling what Sven had said. If Marius was the wrong thing, then what was it that was right? Could it be me?

I faltered. Did Sven have feelings for me? More important, did I have feelings for him? I knew how Marius felt, he didn't exactly hide it from me, and I liked the attention he gave me, but there were times when it made me a bit uncomfortable. He was almost too good. It made me wonder how many women he had seduced.

"Rapunzel, are you all right?" Sven's question jerked me back to the present.

"Yes, I'm fine," I said hurriedly.

"You have been staring off into space for the last ten minutes. I was getting worried."

"No, I am fine, just a bit thoughtful." I stood. "I think that I am ready to go find Valerie. She is sure to be wondering where we are." I knew that I sounded like I was lying, but what was there to do?

It took a long time to find Valerie. We asked strangers if they had seen her. These people were little to no help. "Mr. and Mrs. Schultz? Oh, I saw them earlier. They were buying jam," the people would say. Of course, when we got to where they had directed us, Valerie would be just a few steps ahead.

When we did stumble upon them, in front of the fountain, my gaze went first to Giles. What I saw surprised me greatly. Giles was short, fat and old. His hair was either thinning or falling out. He wore thick spectacles. I could not imagine why Valerie would have married him, for she didn't strike me as someone who would marry a man that much older than she was.

"Ah, we finally meet again. I had thought that the three of you had abandoned me. But I do see that you didn't bring me food. Pity," Valerie said, good-naturedly. "Marius, Sven, Rapunzel, I want you to meet my husband, Giles." She leaned close to Giles, and said loudly, "Darling, these are my friends. They are visiting for the day."

Giles scrunched up his face and asked, "What?"

Valerie sighed exasperatingly and repeated, "These are my friends. They are visiting."

Giles nodded absentmindedly. "Good, good."

"He forgot his ear trumpet, we were about to go get it. You go back to enjoying the day. At seven, we will head down to the Justice Building to dance. Meet you there?" Valerie turned to leave.

"Yes, we will be there," I promised.

As Valerie walked away, Giles' arm around hers, I thought I saw her flinch as his skin touched her hand. I decided that it must have been my imagination.

The boys would not decide what to do, which left me to make all of the choices. We went to go watch the next play in the square, another comedy, this one about a servant who had gotten lost in the woods, and accidentally stumbled upon the Queen's secret plan to dress up like a man. It was full of physical humor, as well as a great deal of sly wit that only about half of the audience picked up on. Sven and I laughed in the same places, and Marius sometimes laughed a little, but he did not seem to find it as amusing as we did.

The hours were passed watching plays, eating the free food vendors advertised on the street, and one time, playing music. We had been wandering aimlessly when we came upon a booth in the street, full of musical instruments. The store owner waved us over and invited us to sample the instruments.

I eagerly laid my hands on a flute. When I blew into it, no sound came out. The owner gently adjusted the position of my hands on the flute, and tilted it a little.

"Purse your lips, yes, like that, and blow down," the owner instructed.

I followed his instructions and was delighted to hear a low, pretty sound come out.

Both Marius and Sven tried the flute, but only Sven was able to get any noise to come out. He asked the owner if there was a fiddle he could try.

When presented with the string instrument, Sven lit up and stroked it softly with a bow. A light chord slipped out. He adjusted it, and began to sing:

> "There was a youth, a well-beloved youth,
>
> And he was the esquire's son,
>
> He loved the Bayliff's daughter dear
>
> That lived in Goadliton."

He gestured to me to continue. My voice replaced his for the next four lines.

"She was coy, and she would not believe

That he did love her so,

No, nor at any time she would

Any countenance to him show."

Sven rejoined me for the next stanza:

"But when his friends did understand

His fond and foolish mind,

They sent him up to fair Dapel,

An apprentice for to bind."

He bowed to the cheering throng of people watching and handed the fiddle back to the owner, grandly praising the instrument. He waved a hand at me and bowed again. I curtseyed, only a little unsteady.

I knew why he had chosen that song. He was trying to get me to remember when I had sung before. Both songs were old common ballads. Both were about love gone wrong, at least at first. Both songs were sung as a duet between the two of us.

Marius clapped lightly, almost mockingly to Sven. He seemed pleased by my performance, but not at my partner. I decided that I did not care. I was allowed to sing with whomever I wanted to sing.

Sven pulled me away towards a small building, a grin on his face.

"Where are we going?" I asked, gesturing for Marius.

"I spotted it as we searched for you," he said.

"But where are we going?"

"It's a surprise," he said, knowing that it was going to bother me to no end. He refused to give me any more information.

We stopped in front of a shop. It blended in with the others, painted drab colors and unkempt. I walked in slowly, and gasped. There were books, nothing but books. I couldn't see where the shelves ended in the musty light.

"What is this?" I tried unsuccessfully to not gawk.

"A bookstore. I thought that you might like it." Sven smiled and walked forward, brushing his fingers against the spines. I moved to join him.

Marius, on the other hand, hung back. He had a look of skepticism as he surveyed the collection that quickly changed to a smile when he saw me watching him. "Come on Marius. Just a few more minutes," I promised.

He shrugged and nodded, settling down onto a small square bench.

I pulled out a large selection and mentally reminded myself to only take a few minutes. We would leave soon. But soon I was engrossed in what I was reading, and minutes turned to hours.

CHAPTER SEVENTEEN

The clock clanged seven times. I looked around to stare at it. Could it already be seven?

"Come, the Justice Building awaits," said Marius, a little too eagerly.

I refused both men's arms and walked side by side with them to the large, white marble building. It loomed over the town menacingly. I did not like to walk directly into its menacing jaws, but I didn't protest. I did not want to seem foolish in front of Sven. He probably went into buildings like this all of the time.

The inside was considerably more inviting. Already, people were streaming in by the dozens. There was a long room off to the side with food, but what held my gaze was the large dance hall with an enormous crystal chandelier hanging from the ceiling.

There was no need to look for Valerie, she found us.

"Oh good, Rapunzel, your hair is still perfect!" she squealed.

"Thank you," I said, not quite sure of the appropriate response.

"Now, before I let you loose, I am going to impose one more rule on you tonight," she informed me.

"What rule?"

"If any gentleman asks for a dance, you will oblige him. Tonight is the night to enjoy what everyone has to offer." She winked in a conspiring way and left.

"In that case, I am going to steal you for the first dance," Sven said. "That is, if you would not mind," he shot to Marius. Without a moment's hesitation, Sven swept me onto the dance floor.

It was a quick, lively dance. We twirled and spun together, laughing heartily. When I danced with Sven, we moved as one. He was leading, but I knew exactly what he was going to do and it was difficult to decipher who really was in charge.

"Are you enjoying your first festival?" Sven asked.

I could not answer immediately because the dance required us to separate briefly. When we came back together,

I said, "Yes. On one thing I am confused however. Could you help?"

"Most likely, I think."

"What is it that we are celebrating?" I had wondered this all day.

"I have absolutely no idea," Sven said, laughing. "I have been to Tia before and frankly, it has always been a bit backwards. I highly doubt that any of the residents are sure about what they are celebrating. They just go along with tradition."

"I do not believe that." I said, not actually sure. I had seen some strange things in this town.

"No, it's true. About two hundred years ago, the Governor had ridiculously extravagant parties thrown for his birthday. He did this for twenty-five years. When he died, for the next four years, the people still celebrated his birthday because that is what they had done for so long. They often refuse to budge from even the most absurd traditions." He paused. "Just like the king."

"No dwelling on anything sad. That is my rule. Tonight, we will be happy. William is still all right. I can feel it." I rubbed the arm I held with my left hand lightly.

The song ended, and Marius interrupted us.

"And now it is my turn. If you do not mind, of course," Marius said, raising his eyebrows mockingly.

Sven bowed graciously and backed off. I saw him go and ask another girl to dance. The girl had been sitting alone, sadly observing the dancers, but not participating herself. She glowed when he grabbed her hand and lead her to the dance floor. I was glad that he had asked her.

"You look dazzling," Marius whispered in my ear. "You are the most beautiful woman in the room without even having to try."

I smiled as we danced. This dance was slower than the previous, and we were closer. I was aware of Marius' every breath.

"I wanted to ask you before, but I wanted to get you alone. Is your hair's extraordinary length why you keep it hidden?" he asked, letting go of my hand to stroke it.

"Well, not at first, that was not the goal. I just needed a way to keep it off the ground, and there was no way that I was going to be able to put it like this all alone. The bag was the only way I could think of keeping it from dragging. I'm glad I did, for a while at least. I don't like the way some people are staring." I reached up to feel my hair, but Marius caught my hand. He pressed it to his lips firmly, staring in my eyes. We had stopped dancing. I had not even noticed.

The song must have ended a while ago, because suddenly I heard a new melody. I backed away. "I am going to go get myself some refreshments, I think." I ran away before he could stop me.

This was all too confusing. I almost missed the simple day to day life I had enjoyed in the tower. Almost, but not quite.

I didn't go to the refreshment table, but to an empty corner. I saw Marius grab a tall glass from one of the servants. I knew that it was probably alcohol. He took a swig and drank the entire glass in one gulp. I shuddered.

Many men asked me to dance soon. Some were quite handsome. One stepped on my toes, but he had such a shy countenance, I did not want to add to his discomfort by pointing out his folly. One of the braver men had a large mustache that twitched whenever he talked. I asked about it.

"This old thing?" he asked. "I decided to grow this because I had trouble thinking of anything to say to women."

"And how does this help you?" I eyed him carefully.

"It has become my greatest conversation starter. See? It has already worked. At this point, you may either back away in fear of insanity on my part, or we can continue this absurd discussion," he said.

I decided that I liked him. "I will stay for the discussion, I think."

That was not the only pleasant conversation I had. In fact, there were many men that I enjoyed dancing with. Every once in a while, I passed Sven, but I had lost sight of Marius.

As the clock was striking nine o' clock, I found myself back in Sven's arms. His hair was a bit disheveled from dancing, and his cheeks were red, but I thought that it made him look even more charming than normal.

"How have you been faring in my absence?" he asked. "I saw you with some very attractive dance partners."

"Stop teasing me. Do not act as if you have been standing alone. You have been dancing the night away just as I have. Have you been enjoying yourself?" I asked.

"Only if you have, Rapunzel," Sven said.

"I have been enjoying myself."

"Then I have too."

I shook my head at the oddity of the conversation. "I am glad. But now I am tired. Please, let me go sit."

Sven led me to a chair. "Rest your feet, you still have until midnight to enjoy yourself. Do not forget that." He left, but I noticed that he did not go and find a new girl with whom to dance.

Though my feet hurt, I did not want to sit still. Instead, I began to wander the building. As I walked down a hall, I realized that I had become lost. Everything looked the same. I turned left, and found myself in an identical hall as before.

I turned another corner and saw Valerie, locked in a passionate embrace with a man. The man was not Giles. They did not see me, too preoccupied with their present activity. My mind raced, and I did what seemed logical. I started to back away, but my heel hit a chink in the floor. It made a small sound that grew large in the enclosed space.

The two broke apart quickly. When Valerie spotted me, she gasped.

"This is not what you think!" she exclaimed.

The man pulled her close again. He looked to her. "Why should we keep it a secret any longer?" He kissed her neck, silencing anymore intended protests.

Frightened about what I saw, I turned and ran becoming even more lost. I stopped and tried to figure out which way I needed to go. I saw a thin hall. Perhaps it would lead somewhere useful. I turned down it and ran into someone, screaming softly when a pair of hands grabbed me and pushed me down the hall. When the light moved over the owner of the hands, I saw it to be Marius. I sighed in relief.

"Oh Marius, I thought that you were somebody else," I said, briefly leaning my head on his shoulder.

"Yes, I can see that," he slurred.

I looked up at him. His face was a bit red, but I did not think it was from dancing. I had not seen him dance with anyone other than me. He had been off by the edges of the room all night, always with a glass in his hand.

"Marius, have you been drinking?" I asked, pulling away a bit.

"Not that much, I am fine," he said. "You look scared." He examined my face carefully. "Is this about what you saw with Valerie?"

"I guess so."

"Do not be surprised. Things like this happen all the time. Valerie is not happy with Giles, so why should she not go and spend time with a man who satisfies her needs?" Marius asked.

"I don't know. I thought that once a woman meets a man who she loves, they stay with each other forever.

Happily ever after and all that." The outside world was becoming more and more like what Jacqueline had always warned me about.

"Happily ever after? Love?" Marius laughed. "Stop living in a fairytale, Rapunzel. Open your eyes. Valerie married Giles for his money and power. He's sickly; and when he dies, she will inherit all of his money and she will then be free to be with that other man."

"I just does not seem right to me," I muttered. I sounded so naïve, but I did not want to go against what I felt. Marius had to be wrong, didn't he?

Marius laughed again, a cold mocking sound. He put one hand around my waist and reached into his pocket with the other. He pulled out a bottle and held it up with a mischievous look. "Care for a drink?"

I frowned at the bottle of clear liquid. "No, thank you."

Marius shrugged and leaned his head back to down much of the bottle. I shivered at the amount he drank.

"That's better," he said, shaking his head. He looked even more intoxicated. "Rapunzel," he said thickly. "Have I ever told you how beautiful you are?"

"Yes, you have."

"I will tell again. You are beautiful." He leaned forward, and I felt his breath in my hair. "You are beautiful, and I am handsome, we do make a good pair, don't you think?"

I didn't answer. Marius was making me extremely uncomfortable, but I could not back away. His grip on my waist was too strong. This seemed all too similar to the man who had cornered me when Sven was at the inn. Only this time, there was no little girl to tell Sven that something was wrong.

"I always said that you were very mysterious, and you still are. I say we get to know each other a little better," Marius hissed.

Without warning, I was spun around and pulled to him, my back to his chest. I felt his breath down my neck, and one of his hands still held tight around my waist. I heard the bottle he had been holding drop and the hand that had been holding it clamped itself around my mouth, effectively cutting off the scream I had been mustering.

Marius began to whisper in my ear. I squirmed to get away from the things he said. At my protests, he would merely laugh and kiss my neck, my hair, my back.

Although I was almost paralyzed by fear at first, my instincts took over as they always did. I lifted my foot and kicked back as hard as I could, hoping to hit something, anything. I did hit something, and by the sound Marius made, it was something painful. For once I was glad for the heels I had been forced to wear.

As soon as his grip loosened even a bit, I broke free and began to run. My shoes came loose and fell off, making me stumble. I tried to speed back up, but Marius was so much faster. He must have jumped to get me, for he sent the two of us flying. I hit the ground hard. The marble burned my skin as I slid.

"You are not going to get away from me that easily, dearie," he said harshly. "Come now, surely you have felt the same way as I have."

He grabbed my wrists in one hand and yanked me up. The other hand found its way around my neck. I was shoved to the wall as Marius leaned forward again. His lips were hard against mine. I tried moving my head away, but with the wall behind me, there was nowhere to go. When I did not return his passionate kiss, Marius pulled back.

"Come on Rapunzel, give in, you know you have imagined this moment," he said in a low breath.

"No, I haven't. Get away, Marius," I said, trying not to breathe in through my nose. The smell of alcohol on his breath was awful.

Marius slapped me hard, leaving a stinging feeling on my cheek. I cried out. Marius went back to kissing me, this time so forcefully, that I couldn't shout for help. His body pressed against me. I struggled against him, but I had never realized just how strong he was.

After a minute, the hand around my neck moved to my back to fumble with the laces on my dress. This time, I did get the energy to scream. My scream was cut off when Marius punched my face, cutting my lip. Blood filled my mouth. Marius shoved me harder against the wall and pushed me up until my feet we almost off the ground. My face was now level with Marius'. The way he held me was painful and I struggled now both against the pain and his hand on my back.

Just when I thought that it was hopeless, that I would not be able to get away, a large hand grabbed Marius' hair and jerked him back.

As Marius let go of me, I fell to the ground like a discarded sack of flour. I looked up and was sure that I was hallucinating, because what I saw could not have been possible.

Sven wrestled furiously with Marius. My head had hit the wall quite hard, so I was not sure if what I saw was real or not. Marius got his hands around Sven's neck, but Sven threw him over his shoulder.

I tried to stand, not completely expecting to be able to and being surprised when I could.

Marius and Sven were about evenly matched. Sven was taller, but Marius had obviously been in more brawls. He knew how to use everything to his advantage. Instead of continuing to go after Sven, however, Marius ran to me and yanked me in front of him. He stood on both my feet so that I couldn't kick him, wrapped one arm all the way around me, pinning my arms to my side and pulled a knife out of his jacket. Why would he have a knife? Had he been expecting something like this to happen?

"All right, Sven. Calm down. It's been fun but it's over now. We're done. I win," Marius said, pressing the knife to my neck.

"No, it's not, Marius. She doesn't want you. Just let her go, and we'll all walk away from this in one piece. How's that sound?" Sven spoke soothingly, like he was trying to calm down Bruce, not a man holding a knife.

"She does want me! Don't you, darling?" He stroked my neck with the knife. I squeezed my eyes shut tight. If I could not see it, it couldn't be real, right? Wrong. Marius continued. "She just doesn't know what I could do for her. What? Did you think that you would be able to sweep her off her feet tonight?" He laughed. "You know nothing about women."

"Just let her go. This is about you and me, isn't it?" Sven took a step.

"Stop right there, are you trying to get her killed?" Marius asked sharply, pressing the blade harder to my throat.

Sven froze. He looked at me carefully, and pulled out his sword. Of course he had his sword with him. I hadn't even noticed before.

I felt the knife dig a little into my skin. Marius was getting jumpy.

I caught the look in Sven's eye and seemed to know immediately what I must do. It was risky, testing whether or not Marius was willing to cut me, but it was the only thing I could think of.

I went limp for a moment; the knife bit me softly. Then I pulled myself down with as much strength as I had.

Marius pulled the knife away to stop from slitting my throat. He had just bent over me when Sven rushed forward and struck him on the head with the broad side of his sword. Marius collapsed on top of me.

Sven pulled me away from Marius' unconscious body. He looked at me sadly.

"Was I too slow?"

Tears filled my eyes. I wanted to tell him that he wasn't, but all the adrenaline that had kept me moving drained away. Now I was just a scared little girl. I almost fell because my feet wouldn't support me. Sven put his arms behind my back and legs, picked me up carefully and started to quickly walk out of the hall.

I buried my head in his chest, trying to block out the images of what had almost happened.

"How did you know that I was here?" I asked.

"The same way I found out last time. A woman came up to me and told me what she had seen. She was too afraid to interfere herself, but she ran to find me until she was out of breath," Sven said.

"What was her name?"

"Ava. She said that she was one of Valerie's seamstresses. She left to the inn and her mistress' house to get our things. She should be waiting for us," Sven said as we twisted through the halls.

We must have gone out a second way, for we never emerged into the great hall. Instead, I found that we had made our way outside. The stars twinkled silently; trying to reassure me that everything was well. They lied.

Bruce and Resa waited for us. Resa wasn't properly saddled, however. Her reins were tied to Bruce's saddle bags. I was going to ride with Sven.

He carefully lifted me up onto the horse and quickly mounted behind me. I looked over and saw Ava, Penny, Beth, and Melody standing off to the side. They all curtseyed. Penny stepped forward. "We will make sure that Mister Marius does not know which direction you went in."

I did not have the voice to say 'thank you' out loud, so I had to say it with my eyes. I was sure by their expressions that they understood.

Sven nodded gratefully to them. "Thank you for everything." He dug his heels in urgently and Bruce shot off, perhaps sensing that time was of the essence.

I had expected that Sven would not want to speak as we rode, but I guessed wrong.

"You know, I thought that you had said that you didn't want to have to rely on me, and that's why I finally agreed to teach you to sword fight. Not that you were any good at it," he teased.

His light mood helped lift the dark cloud that had settled on my mind. "I had it under control. A few more moments and he would have fallen prey to my master plan. You did not need to interfere." The words made me feel a bit better. It was better to pretend I really had been all right. The tears still flowed.

But Sven could not pretend anymore. "I see." He drifted into silence. The silence scared me. I did not want any time to think. Nothing good would come to mind when there was not anything to distract me.

The pessimistic voice that had plagued me for so long broke free of its corner in my mind and seemed to take over. *You always knew that you were worth nothing. You don't deserve kindness. Sven doesn't feel for you the same way that you do for him. He said it himself. He is a gentleman, a chivalrous man. He is merely being polite.*

I closed my eyes and started to hum to myself as a defense to my own thoughts. I was going mad, I was sure. I had crossed that fine line from quirky to insane.

"Rapunzel." The whisper made me think immediately of Marius. I cried out and started to hum louder, anything to make the voice go away. "Rapunzel." When a hand touched my shoulder, I cried out and recoiled, humming louder. "Rapunzel!"

I suddenly realized that it wasn't Marius. It was Sven. I didn't open my eyes, but I relaxed. I was safe. I would always be safe with Sven.

"You know why I worked so hard to get in the tower, did you ever wonder?" Sven asked.

I nodded. I had wondered that for a long time, but I had been shy to ask, a little afraid of the answer.

"When I first heard your voice coming from the tower, I was sure that I had died. There was no way that a sound that beautiful could be coming from any creature on this earth. Or so I thought. When I heard Jacqueline call your name, and I realized who you were, I knew that I had be allowed to meet you again. I was gone from the first note. When I saw you, I realized that you were much more beautiful than I could have hoped." Sven paused. His hand rubbed my arm softly. It was nothing like Marius' touch. It was hesitant, seeming to ask my permission. He did not force any feelings on me. He had never done anything like that.

"I do not believe that for one moment, I'll have you know," I croaked out.

"You are always the skeptic. Why can't you seem to accept that you could perhaps end up happy?" Sven asked.

I wanted to answer, but I did not trust myself to speak, so we rode in a silence that spoke a thousand words. I wasn't refusing to accepting happiness, was I?

We reached another town just as Bruce was beginning to slow, foam gathering at the corner of his mouth. Sven borrowed a horse from a local farmer in order to give Bruce and Resa a rest. He told the farmer that he would have the horse back the next afternoon. We kept on riding, through the night, and into the morning. I fell asleep after not too long, and awoke as Sven lifted me off of the borrowed animal. I panicked when I saw his dark hair, but his light eyes reminded me that he was not Marius.

"Rapunzel, I don't trust you to climb. I am going to pull you up, all right?" Sven asked.

I nodded. I knew that he was right. There was not a chance that I would have the energy to haul myself up. I stood still as Sven tied a loop in the rope. He had me sit in it.

The trip up to the window took longer than normal, and I was vaguely afraid that I was going to fall, but no real emotion registered. When I reached the top, I pulled myself into the room. Sven followed, only a few moments behind me. He picked me up and sat me down on a chair at the table.

"Let me go to bed, I don't want to stay up any longer," I protested.

"No, you need to get some food in you first. Then I will let you sleep." Sven brought out an apple and a slice of bread.

I limply picked up the bread. It did not look appealing at all but I bit into it, if only to make Sven happy.

Sven sat by and made sure that I ate. He encouraged me when I put down my food. When he was convinced that I had eaten enough, he helped me stand, picked me back up and carried me to my bed.

"I think that I am going to sleep in here, if that is all right. I'll go to the other side of the room, but I don't want to leave you alone," Sven said.

"Yes, please stay." My eyes could not stay open.

Sven must have slept without a blanket, for I did not think to offer him one until I was on the threshold of sleep. I did not worry too much. He would be fine. Jean Claude was sure to cuddle up with him. He had always liked Sven just a bit better.

When I woke, it was the middle of the afternoon. I was still exhausted. I imagined that I could have slept for hours more, but Sven's presence kept me up. I looked around to find him on the other side of the room, giving Jean Claude a hearty belly rub.

I stood and went into my closet to change. I had never changed out of the green dress from the night before. When I looked at the bracelet on my wrist, I breathed in sharply. It was thrown into the corner, roughly. I hoped that I might dent or otherwise damage it, but I was not strong enough. I changed into slacks and a loose, comfortable blouse. I cursed the buttons as I fumbled with them. Because my hair was so long, everything I wore had to lace or button up. My fingers just seemed to refuse to work at first, but finally I got them all buttoned. I did not much care what Sven thought at the moment. Anyway, he had once told me that I should have been wearing pants.

Finally I unpinned my hair, letting it fall in waves. The familiar form of my hair at my feet made me feel back to normal.

When I emerged, Sven stood and walked to me, a cloth in his hands.

"This is for you." He handed the cloth to me. It covered something heavy. "It's my dagger. It matches you perfectly. Your eyes and your hair, you see. I do not think that I will ever fit in as Crown Prince, but you fit with who you are."

"Are you leaving?" I asked, holding the dagger close.

"Yes. I think that would be best. Jacqueline will look after you, I am sure. She has taken great care of you so far, and she will continue to do a fine job." He started to leave.

I knew that if I did not act quickly, I was going to lose Sven forever, and I feared that more than anything. I couldn't fathom how I had not been able to choose between Marius and Sven before. Sven overshadowed Marius completely. He was smarter, kinder, and more handsome. I thought. Could this be love? I was not sure, but if this was not love, what was?

"Wait! Sven, don't leave," I said. "There's something, I need to know. Something that I have to find out for myself." I stepped closer to him.

"What? What is it?" he asked.

"Do you love me?" It was a dangerous question, I knew, but I could not hold it back.

"Rapunzel, I don't know that this is the time, so soon after Marius..." He stopped, unable to find words for a moment. "Maybe I should come back–"

I could not wait for him to come back. I needed to know now. Even as he tripped for the right words, I rushed forward and kissed him.

Sven's lips were tender, soft, giving. He had been surprised and tense at first, but he soon returned the kiss just as earnestly as I. All the time we had spent together had been building up to this. I pulled away and looked carefully at him.

"Is that a yes, then?" I asked in a whisper.

"A yes? Of course it is. That was never in question. I have always been in love with the girl in the tower. I have been waiting for you to come around, so I suppose that my wish has come true. What took you so accursedly long?"

"I'm not sure. I had to grow up, perhaps?"

"Yes, that must be it. Someone had to knock some sense into you before I got stuck with you for life." Sven shook his head. "I can only pray that someone will knock some sense into me."

"Oh goodness, no, that wouldn't do at all. If suddenly you start making sense, I may just fall out of love with you." I took a step away.

"You're right. That simply would not do. But for now, I would love to talk some more, but I have to go if I am to get that kind man's horse back by when I promised." He started back towards the window. "Don't go anywhere. When I get back, I have a very important question for you." He climbed onto the ledge.

"Where are earth do you think that I am going to go?" I called.

"I never seem to know with you. That is my blasted problem. If I had you figured out, I would have swept you away to my castle long ago. I will be back in a few days, there are some things that I have to take care of," he said and left my sight.

A voice inside asked me about Marius. I laughed and thought, *Marius who?*

I stood alone, hugging my arms around myself, eyes closed. So this was how love felt. I had wondered all my life and I finally knew. Love was warm, soft, and comfortable. It was like a thick blanket wrapped around me on a cold winter's day. It was a feeling that completely banished the angry voice in my head. Nothing could be wrong. Everything was right. I spun a few times, and then collapsed onto my bed.

I was in love, and Sven loved me back.

Jean Claude jumped onto my stomach. He seemed to understand the feeling of elation that tickled my stomach. I absentmindedly scratched behind his ear. How could it be that I had seen such awful things only hours ago? At this moment, everything was right.

CHAPTER EIGHTEEN

I was never quite sure how long I slept. I could have fallen into an enchanted sleep like so many characters in my books, and I still would not have known. It was Jean Claude who woke me up in the end. He was tired of waiting for me to rise from my slumber.

I sat slowly, and picked him up to place him on my lap. "Oh hello, Jean Claude. What day is it?"

Jean Claude did not know, or he just did not want to talk to me. He held a stick in his mouth. I threw it out the window. Jean Claude scurried to his tunnel.

My vision lost the film that it always acquired during sleep. To my surprise, I found that the day was not about to begin, but about to end. The sun was just about to set behind the mountains.

I stood and wandered over to my mirror. My hair was a mess. Then again, it always was a mess. I still had my necklace on. I carefully unclasped it and set it on the table. I was in slacks and the loose shirt from before. I changed into a nightgown. I did not plan on seeing anyone, and even if I did, I did not feel like wearing anything but the most comfortable piece of clothing I could think of.

Jean Claude began to bark uncontrollably outside the tower. I frowned. It was not like Jean Claude to bark much. Normally, the only things that he barked at were my socks. What could have upset him so much?

I decided to let it go. Jean Claude was a fickle dog and I was too happy to be bothered. I thought of Sven. When would he be back?

The bed invited me back, and I accepted, getting under the covers. I smiled to myself as I thought of Sven. I closed my eyes. If I could get some more sleep, perhaps I would be able to speak some sense when Sven arrived.

I could not get to sleep, however. Something was making me uneasy. Jean Claude had stopped barking, but he did not come up the tunnel. I whistled and called for him, but he still did not appear. He must be on the trail of a squirrel. He loved the animals and could chase them for hours.

A shuffling made me sit up. It was coming from outside the window. I stiffened. This was just the same thing that had happened when Sven had snuck into the tower. This time, however, it couldn't be Sven. He would not sneak up in the middle of the night, not anymore. Who else could it be? A name crept into my mind: Marius.

I yelped softly. It could not be Marius. He could not have found me. I was free of him. He was in the past. I never needed to worry about him.

Dark had fallen faster than I would have wished. There was almost no light to see by. I should have gotten up to light a candle, but I was too petrified to move.

A dark shape appeared in the window and I screamed. However, when the shape tried to enter, it bounced back as if it had hit an invisible wall. It fell and I heard something hit the ground.

My legs suddenly worked again. I rushed to the window just in time to see a man run into the forest, looking back as he went. A rope was attached to a hook. I pulled it off and let it fall. I did not want it in the tower with me. I looked down a bit more and with horror, saw Jean Claude lying at the foot of the tower, unmoving. Even as I watching though, he sat up, shook his head, picked something up from the ground and started up the tower.

When he got to the top, I pulled him to me. I had been so afraid for a moment, but Jean Claude looked just fine. Wait, no he didn't, blood spotted his muzzle. Upon further inspection, I found that the blood wasn't his. I also found a bit of cloth wedged in between his teeth. I realized that Jean Claude had bitten the mysterious man's pant leg. He must have gotten kicked in the head.

Jean Claude squirmed out of my embrace and wandered over to something he had dropped. I wrestled it from his jaws. It was a hat. My eyes widened and I dropped it. It was not just any hat; it was the hat Marius had worn when I had last met with him in the market in Acada.

Panic took hold. I had to leave. He had found me. I threw on some pants and a long sleeved tunic. I grabbed a knee length traveling jacket as well, another piece of clothing that had no purpose for me until I had left the tower. Sven's knife found a home inside the jacket, carefully positioned so that it would not accidentally stab me. I finally reached over and grabbed my necklace. It would help me find my way to Sven.

I had to get away. If I could go far enough, Marius would not be able to find me.

I looked around for anything else that I would need. Money. I would need money sometime or another. To my surprise, I reached into the jacket pocket and pulled out a handful of coins. The jacket must have belonged to Jacqueline. When had she left it here? She had to have much more hidden away to not notice the absence of these coins.

I was about to tie a rope around the hook outside the tower when the fear drained out of me. I must be mistaken. This hat could not be Marius'. There must be hundreds of hats like this. I was overreacting. Even as I thought this, I knew that it had been Marius' hat. It had the same small feather in the band. It was a trivial detail, but it stuck out in my memory. I still had to run away, but I was almost too afraid.

There was a smell of vanilla beans in the air. Jacqueline appeared behind me. I jumped and spun, my heart sinking at what I saw. Jacqueline's normally straight hair was unkempt, and in places it looked like someone had cut it unevenly. I remembered her telling me about spells that required the caster's hair to work. Her clothes were wrinkled and looked as though she had not changed out of them for several days.

Her eyes were large and wild; they were bloodshot as if she had not slept in days. I backed away. She did not look as if she were in her right mind.

"Are you going somewhere?" she asked.

"I– I–" I took another step back.

"Are you going to rejoin the man you have been running off with?" she asked, stepping close to me.

Blood drained out of my face, I felt cold all over. How could she have found out?

"Surprised at what I know? I came back two nights ago and you were nowhere to be found. What I did find, when I came up to investigate was this painting." She pointed at my portrait from Sven. I had not thought to hide it. "It's signed with a man's name at the bottom." She glared at me, absolutely furious. "What is the meaning of this?" she demanded.

"I wanted to tell you, I really did. Sven isn't bad like you said men always were," I said, pleading.

"Wait a moment, Sven? Wasn't that the cursed boy from the village?" I nodded. "And now he has–" Jacqueline started to cry. I rushed forward and hugged her. I knew Jacqueline was not a bad person. She was unhinged, but a good person, with feelings. "He has come to take you away from me. You were never happy here," she sobbed.

"No, I love you. I was very happy," I said.

"I was never enough. You always had that look on your face when you were at the window. You never understood that I was just trying to keep you safe, to keep you with me."

"I knew–"

"Didn't you ever listen to anything I said? It's not safe outside of these walls. I could not stay inside, but you could. Why could you not be content here? People are cruel and dark. They only seek to cause pain. Men are even worse. They want nothing more than to use you," she cried, stroking my hair.

"Perhaps that is right about some people," I said, thinking about Valerie and Marius. They were the kind of people she was talking about. "But I was only out a few days and I learned so much. There are plenty of good people out there, and yes, some of those people are men. If only you would let me go and meet them!" I said.

"Rapunzel, you do not know what I have gone through to keep you safe!" She stopped yelling for a moment, her shoulders sagging. "You are the only family I have left." Her eyes met my own, a spark of anger growing within them. "I had a daughter of my own, you see. She died when she was barely walking. But then I had you to love me. I knew that I could never let you go. So I took you here. What could go wrong? You were where I could always find you. There was no one to hurt you; no one could get in without the magical protection your hair gave you. You would never be infected with the evils of the world.

"But some way or another, you still managed to betray me. That's why I needed the spell to get my magic back; then I could take you away from here and still keep you safe." Her speech was degrading into babbling. "I knew you didn't love it here, but it wouldn't have been forever." She suddenly reached to her hair. "I've done so much. You cannot even imagine what I've done. I sacrificed everything I had for you, and you will stay here with me!"

"No, Jacqueline. It is time that you start treating me like the woman I am. You cannot keep me inside of this tower forever," I said.

Jacqueline's voice transformed from being hysterical with sadness to anger. "If that is what you want, then that is what I will give you. I was never enough for you, you ungrateful little– is that his?" She snatched Marius' hat from me. I had forgotten that I had been holding it. She sneered and shoved it at me. I stumbled back at the force of her push. She grabbed a pair of scissors from the table and held them to my hair. "Take your souvenir of your precious Sven. He will never see you again, I guarantee that!" She repositioned the scissors at the bottom of my ears. They made a loud snipping sound as they sliced through my hair.

I had imagined what it would feel like to cut off my hair many times, but I could not have comprehended the feeling that came. Before, I had never been able to feel the weight of my hair, but now, suddenly, I felt that weight lift. The shock was so great that I screamed. I was afraid. My braid fell to the ground like a dead body. I looked in Jacqueline's eyes and saw madness so great that I screamed again and backed away from her.

I had misjudged how close to the window I was. I fell backwards and down towards the ground. I thought that I was going to die, but I slowed before I hit the ground. I knew that Jacqueline had saved me, but she had not forgiven me.

I stood and she was right beside me. "Leave my sight," she hissed. I turned and started to run, my legs trembling. "Never come back!" she shouted. "Never come back, Rapunzel!"

I shoved the hat in my pocket and ran faster. I should have let it go, but I couldn't. I needed it to remind me how naïve I had been. It was not long before I had to stop. I could not breathe and I had no idea where I was in the dark. I rested for a few minutes and looked back. Jacqueline had been driven mad. I feared to go back, and I feared for Sven even more. I had to try and find him. I knew that it was probably hopeless.

I stood back up to continue on, hoping that I was walking towards Acada. I did not get far. I was walking in pitch-black darkness on uneven ground. It was a rock that foiled my plan to continue moving. I hit my head on the ground, but I did not feel the pain.

CHAPTER NINETEEN

Sven rode towards the tower. It was morning, the sun shone happily. He held a bouquet of flowers in his hand, daylilies of every color, my favorite flower. He wore nice clothes and his crown, odd, since he had resented it so much before.

He stood at the base and called out, "Rapunzel, Rapunzel, let down your hair!"

A golden braid tumbled down the stones of the tower, just as he knew it would.

He climbed, holding the flowers carefully out to the side so that they would not be crushed. He hummed a little to himself. It was one of the folk songs that I was always singing. That he remembered the melody so perfectly was amazing.

When he reached the window, he put his feet on the ledge and grinned broadly, expecting to see my face smiling just as widely.

The look on his face when he was faced with Jacqueline rather than me was heartbreaking. She grinned insanely at him.

"A prince? You have fallen into a better lot of life since we last met. You should have been content to stay there," she said.

"Where is Rapunzel, what have you done with her, witch?" he asked angrily.

"She got what was coming to her, as will you!" Jacqueline said, and pushed him off the precarious ledge he had perched on.

He fell, probably thinking that he would fall safely onto grass as he had before. This time, however, he looked back in time to see that thorns had magically crept up. He never had a chance to cover his face.

He dragged himself slowly out of the thicket in absolute agony. When he rolled over onto his back, I saw that his eyes had been pierced by the thorns. He breathed heavily. The thorns had broken his fall and saved his life, but had taken his vision.

I woke in a sweat. Tears ran down my eyes. Could what I had seen have been real? I looked down at my necklace, and remembered what it could do. The dream had been real. Sven was blind and alone.

It was about the same time that it had been in my dream, early morning, the birds chirping, dew still on the ground. I set off on my journey again, still not sure which way I was going. I put Marius' hat on, ashamed of my cropped hair. I could only think of Sven. I had to find him. My necklace told me that I was moving in the wrong direction, but I thought that I was close to Acada, and I needed some food and water.

It was not until later that afternoon that I found the town. I entered through the gates and the sun set. The streets were emptying, but I was afraid still of being recognized. I pulled up the collar of my jacket and pulled the hat down low. I headed straight for the tavern. I had not been there before, so there was no one who would recognize me. I would rest a bit, find a map, and start once again on my way.

I sat cautiously at the counter. The man behind it asked me what I wanted. I asked for water and glanced furtively around. To my surprise, I saw the man whose finger I had bitten. His hand was still bandaged.

A stranger came to sit next to me. He kept his head down and his face away, but so did many people in the room, and I didn't think anything of it.

"Two glasses of your finest," he said in a gruff voice. "One for me and one for the lady." He jerked his head at me.

"Oh, no thank you. I don't drink," I said.

"Always the good one, now aren't we? Never willing to break the rules," the man said, taking a swig from his glass.

"I'm sorry, what did you just say?" I asked.

The man turned to me, head still down. "You are always going to be this wonderfully innocent, aren't you?" He raised his head and cleared his voice. Marius laughed. "Oh, I could never bear to let you go, Rapunzel. You must know that by now."

I bolted. As I cleared the door, I did not hear Marius come after me, but I concentrated more on running than listening. I turned down alleys, only succeeding in getting myself more and more disoriented. Once I turned and saw Marius waiting at the end of the alley, waiting casually. I turned, my breath catching in my throat.

I wished more than ever that I could actually run for a reasonable amount of time. I stopped and hid in a doorway. I knelt, trying to catch my breath.

A hand clamped itself over my mouth. I tried to scream, but no sound came out, whether from the hand or a lack of breath altogether, it was hard to tell.

"You really didn't think that you could get away from me, did you?" Marius asked. "I know every inch of this town. I could have followed you all day." He patted my head. "I see that you found my hat. I did not think that I was going to get it back. I thought that dog of yours would have eaten it. Thanks for keeping it safe for me."

I struggled. I could not go through this again. I would not go through this again. I tried to bite his fingers just as I had with the man from before. Marius was smarter than that. He tied a gag around my mouth.

"Rapunzel, Rapunzel," he softly sang in my ear, as he pulled me up. "The girl with the golden hair; the one who said no. Oh, Rapunzel, no one has ever said no to me before. I could not let you be the first, don't you see?" He pulled his hat off of my head. When he saw that my hair was gone, he sighed. "All good things can't last, I suppose." He stroked it. I shivered and tried to move away. His grip on me was far too tight. "This time, you are not going to slip away." He pulled me inside the building we were in front of. The room was lit. A chair was waiting, obviously for me. He sat me down on it. The gag was removed. He must have been certain that there was no one to find me. I could not figure out how he had known where I was going to hide.

"Oh, come on Rapunzel, aren't you going to ask how I did it? How I found you?" Marius paced. "It really does make a good story." He waited for me to ask. I would not, but I wanted to know. "Fine." He pulled a chair up, sitting on it backwards.

"Marius," I couldn't help saying, "Just let me go."

His playful grin disappeared. "Do you know what I went through? There are a few things I suppose you should know. I told you once that I dealt in jewelry, is that right?" I nodded carefully. He laughed. "Well there is some truth in that, but my real medium is life. Someone comes to me, tells me that they need to make someone disappear. For a bag of coins, I can make that happen." I stared in horror. Marius killed people. It's what he did for a living. He continued on, "A woman comes to me, says her name is Jacqueline and that she needs me to hide a man who goes by the name of William. I agreed. That's part of my job description. If someone knows how I deal, they've got to have heard it by word of mouth, and they're bound to be trustworthy, right?" He slammed his fist on a table. "Wrong! This thing turned out to be a lot more complicated than I had originally thought. I had hidden William where no one would ever think to look for him, and everything was going fine, until you and that idiot Sven showed up. The only good thing that happened was when Jacqueline gave me a magic bracelet as payment. It would track whoever wore it."

I stared. My bracelet: That had been how he had found me. "Jacqueline gave you that?"

"Yes, brilliant, isn't it? I was pretty shocked when Philip recognized it. Jacqueline must have been no better than a common thief. One that could use magic, but still." He shook his head in disbelief. "After a while, I knew that you had taken it off, but I could still feel you." Marius grinned, but only briefly. "Things were looking up for me until you mentioned Jacqueline and William. That's when everything connected. I had to keep you away from William at all costs. The deal was off with me and Jacqueline if William was found and I had already spent the extra money she paid me."

I shook my head, everything becoming clear. Furtively I looked for an exit I could escape through. There was only the door that Marius stood resolutely in front of. I thought about what Marius was saying. All of us had been part of a game Jacqueline was playing. No one knew everything that was going on. In the end, even Jacqueline didn't have all the pieces.

"Having an excuse to spend some more time with you was just what I was looking for. When you ran away from the dance, I just followed where the bracelet led me. I have got to admit, I was rather surprised. The mysterious girl with the golden hair became the girl in the tower." I flinched when Marius used the same words that Sven had. "I was terribly disappointed when I could not enter."

"Sven could get in," I said. "He got in easily, all by himself."

Marius' countenance darkened. He picked up a dainty knife from the table and twirled it in his fingers idly. "Ah, yes. Sven." He walked up to me and played with what remained of my hair. "What is it about him that makes him better than me? Sven, with his stupid little accent and his pompous manner, what is so good about him?" He grabbed my arm. "Why do you prefer him over me?" Marius was as wild-eyed as Jacqueline had been. He was slipping.

I didn't answer. I was not going to goad Marius with words.

"It doesn't matter anymore, I suppose. I will have you now." Marius yanked me up.

I thought fast. I was sure that no one was coming to come save me this time. I would have to think of something.

Marius played with the knife on my neck. I reached for it and tried to wrestle it from him. There was no way that I was going to get it, but I did send it flying from his fingers. He was losing his grip on things; he must have been, for normally, I am sure that he would not have hesitated. What matters is that he did though and I used that hesitation to flee the room.

It was just an extension from the chase before, except that this time, I could hear Marius run behind me. I knew what I had to do, but I was afraid. I knew what Marius would do if he caught me, and I was afraid.

But not too afraid to stop what I was about to do. When I knew that I had a few seconds lead, I stopped, pulled Sven's dagger out of my jacket and spun around, throwing it as hard as I could, knowing as soon as the blade spun out of my fingers that it would hit its target.

Marius gasped, the knife embedded in his stomach. I gasped too. It had been as easy as throwing the knife into a tree and that was horrifying.

I walked slowly up to him, ready to bolt in case he reached for me. Marius sunk to his knees, staring at me in wonder.

"You were full of surprises up until the end," he whispered. "I didn't think that you would have the guts."

"You were wrong," I said, keeping a safe distance.

Marius died without any more complaint. He looked like he was in intense pain, and I looked away until his breathing stopped. I stepped carefully over to him and took the knife from his body. I was terrified by what I had just done, but even more so because I didn't feel any remorse. His hat lay abandoned on the ground. I stared at it. I would not forget Marius, but I would not mourn him.

"Goodbye," I whispered.

I had to find William. Jacqueline had taken him, and I could guess why. But where to look? A name suddenly came to mind: Nago. Marius had said that no one counts Nago. It would be the perfect place to hide someone. I ran to the stables.

The stable hand was all too willing to give me Resa and directions to Nago once I had shown him the stack of coins in my hand. I learned from him that it was only a few days away. I knew not to stay in Acada. That decision was obvious. I could not stay, not after Marius…

I rode a few miles away and stopped so that I could sleep under the stars. As I was drifting off, I tried to feel guilt. That was right, wasn't it? I killed a man. I shuddered at the word kill, but that was what it had been, hadn't it? It had been in self-defense, but still. I was worried that it was going to eat away at me.

For two days I rode, following the trail the stable hand had pointed out. It wasn't hard. Every fifty feet or so there was a sign. It was as if someone had anticipated the trails being traveled by a desperate, naïve eighteen year old girl. Even I couldn't manage to get lost.

I passed people often. They gave me food in exchange for gold. Some asked why I was traveling, but I waved them off with vague answers about seeing family. A few offered to give me a place to stay, and one boy even asked me to stay and live with him; I left that house in a hurry.

My thoughts ventured constantly to Sven. I should be looking for him. What if he was lost? What if he was dead? I tried shutting out these unpleasant questions. William could be alive, and it was my fault he was in danger.

On the morning of the third day, I reached Nago. I realized why Marius had said that no one counted it. Plontum, the capitol and only real town was empty and gray. I asked around, and eventually pieced together where Marius and Jacqueline had been.

I made my way to the heart of the town and into the cellar of a large building. I had a candle that one kind soul had given me, but it only gave me a small sphere of light.

"William?" I called. "William!" I did not know how else to find him in the maze of darkness.

There was a muffled sound to my left. I headed that way, and found a man chained to a wall that I supposed was William. There was a thick gag in his mouth.

I rushed forward and pulled the gag away. William opened his eyes with a snap and jerked away. He looked at me and blinked, confused. "Who are you?" he asked, his voice grating due to disuse.

"My name is Rapunzel. I'm a friend of Sven's," I looked around for the keys for the chains. They hung on a hook a few feet away. I unlocked the manacles on his wrists. Will gasped and rubbed them as the blood began to flow through properly.

"Where is Sven?" he asked. "Why isn't he here?"

I started slowly. "I don't know. I'm going to go find him, but I knew that I had to get to you first. Let's go. The faster we leave, the faster I can find Sven."

We sat for a few minutes. William was too drained of strength to move at first, so he began to talk. "She came out of nowhere. One minute I was sneaking away from the kitchens and suddenly something hit me and I woke up here." He rubbed the back of his head absentmindedly. "She came in every few days and took blood." I winced when he showed me his scars. "I just keep thinking that she was going to kill me. After a while, I started hoping that she would kill me. She kept making these potions made of blood, hair and skin and drinking them. When nothing happened, I think she began losing her mind."

I didn't want to hear anymore. "We should go," I said.

"Make sure that you free the other man, too." Will began to stand, wobbling. I looked closer at him. He had blue eyes like the sky and light sandy hair. I had thought that maybe his voice would sound like Sven's, but it didn't. That actually made more sense. William had probably been born in Dao, not Rodia.

"What other man?" I asked.

Will pointed. I turned to see another man, not chained to the wall, but gagged and unconscious.

I walked over and carefully removed the gag. The man did not stir.

"He was here much longer that I. He might not wake," William said softly.

I ignored him. The man would wake. I couldn't leave him like this. Will brought some water in a bucket. I gently dipped my fingers in it and dabbed them on his forehead. Eventually the man began to stir. He squinted up at me and Will.

Something was awfully familiar about him. What was it? I thought about it and inhaled sharply when I realized who he was. It was Emmanuel, the man who had scared Jacqueline so much when he came to visit us. It had been so long ago.

He knew me instantly. "Rapunzel, my child," he breathed. "I never thought that I would see you again."

"What did you call me?" I asked.

"You never put it together? Of course, how could you? You were so small when I last saw you. You have grown up into such a beautiful young woman. Your mother would be so proud." He coughed weakly.

I gasped in shock. "You're my father?"

"Yes, child." Emmanuel smiled. He tried to stand, but couldn't manage.

"I got him." Will picked up Emmanuel and helped him stand. "Let's get out of here."

We had to go slowly. I had so many questions, and Emmanuel–I still tripped over the word "father"–and Will could not walk quickly.

My father spoke swiftly, trying to make up for years of separation in but a few minutes. He spoke of his acts of thievery at first, though he wandered from topic to topic. "I never thought that any harm would come of it. Jacqueline was reserved, especially after her child died. There were a few times that I tried to talk to her, to make her feel welcome, but she always pushed me away. I should have started following you two immediately, but when your mother died–" He couldn't continue.

"What was her name?" I asked.

"Trishna," he said, tears in his eyes.

Hesitantly, I put my arm through his and leaned up against him. We stayed like this for a while. I couldn't to rip myself from him so soon, and he seemed content to stay with me. I didn't forget that I had to go, however.

When it finally came time to part, I instructed Will and Emmanuel to head straight to Dao; I would be going to go find Sven and I would have to leave them.

Emmanuel couldn't get his words out fast enough. "It took a long time, but when I could finally stop mourning, I went after Jacqueline myself. She had surrounded your cottage with spells and for years I couldn't find you. After a long while, however, the spell began to wear off. When I confronted Jacqueline that day, she became frightened and locked you in the tower to keep you away from me and the world." He coughed. "I should have tried harder, but then she locked me down here for so long…" He coughed harder.

"You were looking for me? You didn't just leave me?" I asked.

"Of course not! Why would I?" he asked as we emerged outside.

Both men had to cover their eyes from the bright light of day. I reached Resa and mounted. Will regained vision first and nodded up at me. "Thank you," he said. "I wish you a safe journey. I would come with you, but…"

I understood. They were going to need days of rest before they could even make it out of Nago.

"Goodbye father." I relished those words.

"This is not goodbye, Rapunzel, we will meet again soon, and this time you will be able to introduce this prince who you so obviously care for," Emmanuel said.

I blushed, beet red. Emmanuel could already see right through me.

Will put his hand on my boot. "Wait, I almost forgot to tell you." He looked awfully downcast. "The king is dead. Sven needs to go back as soon as he can. He is no longer the Crown Prince. As the only heir, he is now king. You must find him soon."

"Go to the palace and tell the court that he is coming." I flicked Resa's reins, but didn't nudge her with my heels. I was reluctant to leave Emmanuel. I still had much to ask.

"Go Rapunzel! I will find you," my father promised.

I tossed them a handful of coins for food and set off.

The prompting from the necklace was stronger than ever before. I rode hard. After a few hours, I knew that Resa was tired, but I couldn't let up. We were still so far away. We entered a forest. I was not sure of its name, and I did not care. I had to duck under low branches. It only took one time of carelessness for me to be knocked off of Resa. If Sven had been with me, Resa would have stayed around, but he wasn't, and she ran off. As I lay on the ground, I looked to the side and saw my necklace. It had fallen off, and the beads were all cracked or broken into pieces. I gathered a few of the fragments, but they didn't give me any clue to where I might find Sven. I pocketed them nonetheless.

I almost gave up, but I couldn't. Sven was wandering blind. I had to find him. I had to know what he was going to ask. Now that I had finally realized that I loved him, I couldn't let him go away.

I couldn't continue on any more right then, and I allowed myself a brief rest, closing my eyes and curling into a ball.

CHAPTER TWENTY

I wandered aimlessly for a week without any sign of Sven. I ate what I could find and followed a river so that I would always have fresh water.

> "There was a girl,
>
> A girl in a tower.
>
> She felt nothing,
>
> But there was a Prince,
>
> And he felt everything,
>
> By a twist of fate,
>
> The two were paired together,
>
> The Prince was soon to show
>
> The girl all that she was missing."

My voice broke. "I didn't deserve you, Sven. I had everything that I needed to find you, and I couldn't even do that," I said. The solitude of the woods was much worse than it had been in the tower. I was in danger of losing my mind, just like Jacqueline.

Singing was the only thing that kept me calm. I didn't know where I was, I didn't know where Sven was, and I was going to die alone, in these woods, but I would not stop singing. Every once in a while, I would stop walking, my vision too clogged with tears to continue.

When I heard a scuffling in the woods, I pulled my knife out, and steadied myself. It was too loud to be an animal. I saw the outline of a man and raised the weapon above my head. When the figure emerged, I dropped the knife. It fell heavily to the ground.

"What was that? Rapunzel, is that you? I heard your voice, I heard you sing. Or am I going mad?" Sven asked, turning his head wildly. "Please tell me I'm not going mad."

At first I couldn't move. I couldn't even speak.

"Don't do this to me. Say something," Sven said, eyes wandering. Dried blood still lingered on his face, scratches showing where the thorns had hit.

I ran forward and embraced him tightly. I couldn't make my voice work.

"Rapunzel, is that you?" he asked. I didn't answer. "If it's not, this will be a bit awkward. Please answer, I beg of you."

I nodded into his neck. "It's me, Sven," I cried, tears blurring my vision once more.

With a whoop, he picked me up and spun me around. When he set me down, he felt my face in his hands and kissed me fiercely on the lips. I forgot about anything else in the world. I could have stood there forever in Sven's arms.

His hands made his way up to my hair. He could feel where it had been cut off.

"It really is gone," he said in wonder. "Can you feel the difference in weight now?"

I laughed. "Does it matter?"

"Yes, of course it does. Rapunzel, think about it. If you can feel how much lighter your head is now, that means that I was right."

I laughed again. Sven could never take anything seriously.

"Sven, we have got to go back to the palace. The king is dead. You're king now," I said.

"I don't care. I just want to stay with you." His face was looking at me, but his eyes wandered aimlessly. "I wish that I could see you," he moaned.

"You never listen. It doesn't matter that you can't see me." I kissed him lightly. "I am still here, and that is all that matters, right?"

Sven smiled, but I could tell that the lack of sight was killing him. I wished that I knew how to help him.

I did. I almost hit myself for being so stupid. Once, Jacqueline had restored a man's sight with her magic. I remembered the words, and I thought that it would be worth a shot. Nothing else in my life was going the way I thought, so maybe just this once I could do magic.

I knelt; Sven came with me. He leaned his head against my shoulder, his face still to mine. I didn't tell Sven what I was doing, I just put my face up to his, so that our foreheads were touching and I began to sing the words. Tears ran down my face and onto Sven's as I did so. *Please.* I thought. *If I ever get just one spell, let it be this one. Let this work.* I knew that it was foolish to hope. Why should the spell work? Nothing had ever worked before.

I thought that it might this time, however. Without even realizing it, I put one hand to the shattered necklace in my pocket. I thought that the pieces felt warmer than usual. Jacqueline had said that it had its own magic. I willed it to help me heal Sven's eyes.

Nothing happened for so long that I was afraid that it was not going to work, when Sven stiffened. He pulled away and looked at me. I gasped. He didn't just look in my direction; he was really looking at me. I jumped up at the shock of it.

"Rapunzel?" he asked, astonished.

I didn't answer; I hugged him even tighter than before.

"Rapunzel, what did you do? I can..." He could not finish. He didn't need to.

We stood, embracing each other for a long time. Eventually, we sank to the ground again, Sven sitting with me on his lap. I couldn't stop staring at his eyes. They were like pieces of sunlight.

"You are amazing, you know," he said several times. "I like the hair better now, I think." I was sure he only said this because he knew that it would make me feel better, but I appreciated it.

I just smiled contentedly. I remembered something. "You had something to ask me, don't you remember?" I turned a little to see him better. I couldn't get enough of looking at his eyes and seeing them watch me back.

Sven jumped and pulled himself from beneath me. "Yes, I did." He knelt on the ground and looked at me shyly. "We haven't known each other for very long, and I never took much stock in the whole love at first sight stuff, or at least, I didn't, but I love you." I realized what he was going to ask. "Will you marry me, Rapunzel?"

If I had read this in a book, I would have laughed at it. It would have seemed foolish and sappy. Now that it was real, however, I still laughed but took his hand. "Yes." There was nothing more to say.

"I had a ring, but I lost it when I fell. There will be a ring for you at the palace, but until then I should…" He trailed off, looking distressed.

I cut off his words with another kiss. After a few minutes, I looked at him. "You know, sometime we are going to have to go to the palace," I said.

"Really? And why is that?"

"You're king now, you can't just run away."

"I think that being king is precisely why I can run away. I make the rules, don't I?" He sighed and leaned against me. "Fine, only because you insist."

"Oh I do." I hugged him one more time. "Anyway, I've got to go get my ring," I murmured. We sat there for a long while, prolonging the moment when we would have to return to reality. We did eventually stand and start to walk. It was ridiculous, really. Sven had no better idea of where he was any more than I did. He normally had a great sense of direction, but without his sight, he had wandered in circles until he was completely disoriented.

"Just my luck, eh?" he asked, pulling me close as we walked. "I figure if we walk far enough, we have to come across something, right?"

I laughed, shaking my head. We would be wandering the woods until the end of time. That didn't sound too bad.

We did stumble across something eventually, and I could tell that it was as shocking to Sven as it was to me. It was the tower, my old home. It was much different, however. Vines ran rampant up its sides, bricks were crumbling, and many had already fallen. To my surprise, I saw a door. It had been walled up, but it was falling apart now. After a moment, I supposed that I should have remembered it. It was the way I had entered the tower originally, after all.

Without a word between us, Sven and I entered and precariously climbed the ruined stairs. We emerged in my closet. It was filled with bits and pieces of the stones.

"Well this would have been much more convenient," Sven remarked. I hushed him.

He wouldn't be hushed. "You ever figure out why, or rather how, I was able to get into the tower without your help?"

"Yes. I thought that maybe a part of it was because you have magic in you, your mother being a witch and all." Sven flinched. "And the curse might make you immune to the magic, because really, it was kind of bad luck that you got into the tower," I started.

"Oh? And how do you figure that?" Sven stopped before we got into the main room.

"If you hadn't made it into the tower, you wouldn't have been stuck with me. But the more I thought about it, I realized that there might have been something else to let you through." Sven waited for me to finish. "This whole ordeal has been pretty much told to the book, so what if it was true love?" I asked.

Sven kissed my hand. I love you, Rapunzel. I've been waiting for you all my life," he said. "Come on, let's go." He led me into the main room. I gasped.

My cut hair lay discarded on the ground. The room had been ransacked. Contents of drawers were thrown about, my bed was overturned, tapestries were torn down, and in the middle of the room was my painting, ripped into a dozen pieces. I cried out softly at the sight of it. I crossed over to the shelves and fingered the books. At first I thought that they were fine, but then I pulled one out and saw that they were burned to ashes.

Remembering something, I reached in between the black remains and pulled out a jar. My caterpillar was gone, replaced by a large, beautiful butterfly with rainbow wings. I twisted the lid and tipped the opening to the window. The winged bug flew out of sight.

Sven came over to me and looked about. "Jacqueline wasn't too happy, was she?"

I bit my lip and set the jar down. "Where is she now? Where did she go?"

My question was answered relatively quickly. We found a burned section of the floor surrounded by ash. It smelled like vanilla.

"Burnt herself up," Sven muttered. "I have heard of that happening, when someone uses too much magic all at once."

I buried my head in his shoulder. I didn't want to remember Jacqueline like that. I didn't look back out until we had left the tower.

As we crossed a hill, as the tower faded into the distance, I felt a tug at my heart. I hadn't found what I had been looking for. A small sob tore from my throat. Quickly, I covered my mouth. I hadn't wanted Sven to see me crying. Again.

"What is it?" he asked, looking worried about me.

"Nothing, it's stupid, really." I tried to brush him off.

"Rapunzel, tell me. Something is bothering you."

I shrugged, sniffing. "Jean Claude. I had hoped that I would find him, but I suppose that maybe Jacqueline–" I couldn't finish that sentence so I tried again. "I suppose he left."

The look on Sven's face made me cry harder. "Jean Claude is gone?" he asked. "I thought that you had taken him somewhere. I assumed…" He grabbed my hands. "We will find him. Watch." He let go of my hands and cupped his own around his mouth. "Jean Claude! Where are you, boy?"

It seemed like he was calling for hours. I sat on the ground, trying to stem my sadness. I had given up when suddenly I heard it: a light barking from the distance.

I jumped to my feet. "Jean Claude?!" I cried.

My heart leapt when I saw the familiar puppy stagger towards us. I ran over and scooped him up, carefully, for I saw him limping. He was bleeding a little from his ear, but other than that he was fine. He held a map in his mouth. He had always been so much smarter than he looked.

Now that Sven had his bearing, we started to make much more progress. Jean Claude sat snuggled in my grasp. I didn't want to ever let him go again.

"I don't blame her for anything she did," I said absentmindedly as we walked.

"No?" Sven looked at me.

"I don't think that she had full use of her mind towards the end. She was trying to complete a spell that would give her full use of her magic back. That was why she kidnapped William," I said, holding my hand to his mouth. I would explain it all later. Right now, I needed to puzzle this all out loud. "It all made her rather unstable, I suppose."

It was a good thing that Sven was holding me up, because I didn't think that I would be able to walk by myself.

"Let's not talk about this right now," Sven said, pulling me along faster. "Think about something happy."

"What? Give me a suggestion and I'll consider it."

Sven thought. "You know, if you marry me, you're going to be a queen." He nudged me a few times.

Queen. I had never thought about that. Yes, Sven would be king, he should be king, but I couldn't be a queen. I would just be the King's Wife. I would have my own little title. But queen? No, I never saw myself as queen.

I looked up at him, thinking about what it would be like to sit on a throne and wear a crown.

"I don't think that I would be a good queen. I'll pass. Can I do that?"

"Uh, no. Sorry, you're stuck. You already said yes to me, and now I've got my heart set on you, so you can't back down now. You'd break my heart, you know." Sven frowned in false disapproval. He stopped teasing when he saw how serious I was. "You'll be great."

"Sven, I've been locked in a tower for six years. I don't know anything about running a country."

He took a step back looked at me. "Of course I'm not going to let you run the country! I have a bit more sense than that."

I was quite offended. I didn't think that I could rule a country, but I didn't like that Sven assumed that I couldn't.

He must have been getting better and better at catching the subtle changes in my thoughts, for he said, "That's not what I meant. You will be perfect because you haven't grown up in the kingdom. The people need someone new, someone concerned with things both outside and inside the city." He kissed the top of my head.

This was how it should be. It was a fairy tale ending, or close enough to it anyway. I had found my prince, well, my king, and I loved him. It was not going to be easy, though. Perfect endings weren't real, and honestly, who wanted a perfect man who never did anything wrong? Sven got angry sometimes and so did I. He could not sing and I could not paint. He made fun of me constantly, especially regarding my hair, which I was particularly sensitive of.

I enjoyed all of the quirks that Sven came with. I mean, what was the fun in a man who was afraid to make a fool of himself?

Printed in Great Britain
by Amazon